LAST OF THE SUMMER WINE

Foggy, Compo and Clegg – the famous characters from the popular BBC television series of LAST OF THE SUMMER WINE – are very much the central characters in this novel by Roy Clarke.

It's a whacky, rumbustious yarn told with great zest and skill; and with many laughs on every page as our three heroes try to dispose of the corpse of a friend whose libidinous eyes proved fatally too ambitious.

A north countryman, Roy Clarke has made a great reputation for himself as a screen writer. Before LAST OF THE SUMMER WINE was THE MISFITS and there have recently been many highly acclaimed plays of his on both BBC and ITV. He now hopes to add novel-writing to his list of pursuits. He lives with his wife, son, daughter, two dogs and three cats in a converted windmill near Doncaster.

ROY CLARKE

Last of the
Summer Wine

GRANADA
London Toronto Sydney New York

Published by Granada Publishing Limited in 1983

ISBN 0 586 05903 2

First published in Great Britain
in a slightly different edition by
Hodder Paperbacks Ltd 1974
Copyright © Roy Clarke 1974, 1983

Granada Publishing Limited
Frogmore, St Albans, Herts AL2 2NF
and
36 Golden Square, London W1R 4AH
515 Madison Avenue, New York, NY 10022, USA
117 York Street, Sydney, NSW 2000, Australia
100 Skyway Avenue, Rexdale, Ontario, M9W 3A6, Canada
61 Beach Road, Auckland, New Zealand

Printed and bound in Great Britain
by Cox & Wyman Ltd, Reading
Set in Times

To Enid
who makes it all possible

It was Friday.

The tar was melting on the road outside the TV rentals.

Mrs Beever's Eva was stung on the knee by a wasp as she was sitting on the outside toilet with the door open for the breeze and the view of the park it afforded, being a nature lover.

The bird at the cleaners was rumoured to be wearing sweet very little under her nylon overall.

Some said nothing at all.

But it was the weather for the birth of legend.

The regulars at the Three Legs took their beer out to the pavement.

Micklethwaite's were out of bluebag.

'Though we could have had some,' Micklethwaite said. 'Being the kind of small private business that stocks that kind of low profit line as a customer service, not like them bastard supermarkets.'

For the second time young Byron Pilbeam abandoned O-level English and took his acne and a sports jacket to the cleaners.

At C. W. Moss & Sons, Quality Furnishers, the junior mutinied and went into shirt sleeves.

They even had the heat down at the Electricity Showrooms.

They were watching the fly.

'Neurotic way to travel,' Clegg said. 'If I were green

5

and shiny and had a pair of wings, I'd be inclined to tek things much more slowly.'

With a single finger he tilted his cap forward fractionally to keep the sun from his eyes.

In the full glare of the sunlight the fly lurched giddily through a series of unsatisfactory, soon abandoned, perches.

'They bite,' Compo broke the silence truculently. He rubbed the stubble on his chin in further declaration of his boredom. It sounded like biscuits being eaten.

Foggy shifted uncomfortably on the grass, concerned for the crease in his trousers.

'Some of 'em bite,' Clegg conceded. 'It's understandable. You can't expect anything that size to put all its faith in bloody judo.'

Compo frowned at the fly. It ignored him.

'They used to bring me mam out in lumps,' he said.

Foggy gave him a critical glance. 'From the King's Head – they used to bring your mother out in all sorts of conditions.'

'It's true,' Compo nodded. 'She knew how to enjoy herself did me mam.' He began to list on his tobacco-stained fingers. 'She liked Guinness, black puddin', rhubard and that bus driver from Mythomroyd. What were his name? Gavin or some bloody thing. He din't come from round here. He got a conductress in trouble. He used to let me listen to his watch.'

'What did it used to say?' Clegg enquired.

Foggy supplied the answer. 'Don't go near the bedroom.'

They turned to look at Compo. He was fiddling cheerfully; trying to blow noises from the edge of a blade of grass.

*   *   *

They were up the hill. Sprawled at the foot of a drystone wall. The town barely visible at the end of the valley below them. It was warm enough for Clegg to have abandoned his plastic mac. In a wild summer frenzy of grey flannel trousers and the jacket and waistcoat of an old suit, he was seated now, his glasses on the end of his nose, contentedly leafing through a field guide to the common insects.

'If you had any idea,' Foggy nudged Compo. 'Of how many unseemly substances there are liable to be on that blade of grass, you wouldn't be chomping it with such enthusiasm.'

Compo blew a note of anal music through his lips.

'That's right,' Foggy nodded vigorously. 'It'll be covered in that for a start.' He pointed to the dark-faced sheep grazing on the lower slopes. 'And then we have to consider the secretions of all the various insects.'

'Aw, shut thee face,' Compo said without malice. He selected another green blade with the air of a gourmet.

'There's no justice,' Foggy complained, drawing Clegg's attention from his book and indicating the untidy gnomelike figure of Compo. 'He's idle, unhygienic and smokes too heavy, and he's going to live for ever.'

'I owe it all to Rose Hip Syrup,' Compo smirked. 'And me mam's constant lack of affection.'

'Poor as they were,' Clegg said, looking over his glasses. 'You've got to admit there was always summat on the table. Like the cat or his ferrets.'

'He were brought up on chips.'

'We weren't.'

'You bloody were. It was straight off the breast and down to the fish shop. One of the characteristic noises of my childhood. Him sucking chips.'

'Me granny used to feed us.'

'Aye. Information. So your Wally would know where to lay his hands on stuff.'

'Our Wally used to know exactly where to lay his hands on stuff. He used to creep up and goose 'em from behind.'

'Mebbe he was shy,' Clegg said. 'Could it have been a kind of dumb, inarticulate reaching out for affection?'

'Sounds reasonable,' Compo said.

Foggy snorted.

'I mean it wasn't as if he was indiscriminate,' Clegg continued. 'He only did it to women and young girls.'

Foggy removed his trilby and laid it carefully down. With his handkerchief he wiped perspiration from his neck inside his shirt collar. Then readjusted, by familiar feel, the precise setting of his neatly knotted tie. He frowned at Compo's tatty jacket.

'Must you flaunt your sensuality? Do you think everybody wants to see your elbow poking cheekily through that hole?'

'One of my best features, me elbows,' Compo said, twisting his arm as he tried to examine the effect.

A lark rose ecstatically behind them into the sky. In the distance the vast, bare shoulders of the moors were edged with purple.

'Be a bit warm for Sam this afternoon,' Clegg squinted at the sun.

'It always is in hospital.'

'Aye.'

'He's up and about now. Mebbe they'll let him sit outside.'

'Mebbe so.'

'Anyway. We'll cheer him up tonight.'

8

'Listen!' Foggy said, fixing Compo with an accusing stare. 'This time – don't be saying sod in front of his missis.'

'What's tha talking about?' Compo protested indignantly. 'She wants to be thankful I kept it as mild as sod. I'd just dropped a fag down me wellie.'

'You shouldn't be smoking in the wards.'

'We were there for an hour. What do they expect you to do?'

'They expect you to have a bit of respect for Sam's thrombosis. He's had to give up things like that.'

'They're not consistent about that either,' Compo said. 'If they're trying to cut off everything what's bad for him, what the hell is his missis doing there?'

There was a moment's silence as they each pondered this piece of impeccable logic.

'Mebbe he likes her better now he's been at death's door.'

They looked at Clegg unconvinced.

'Would you?' Compo enquired.

'No,' Clegg admitted. 'But think on, he's still a bit weak.'

'Not in the head,' Compo insisted.

They fell silent again as the rigid, upright, angular figure of Sybil, Mrs Hoskins, loomed large in their minds. It was as if a sudden chill had rippled through the valley.

'She's good wi' pastry,' Clegg said.

'She keeps his house immaculate,' Foggy conceded.

'Aye,' Compo admitted. 'So much so that he spends half his life in the shed.

'She must have been some consolation to him,' Clegg insisted. 'When he was critical. I should think if any

9

mortal thing could mek death seem palatable, Sybil could.'

Below them a car was nosing along the dirt track near the river.

'Well,' Foggy said, 'give Sam his due. He's made the best of it. Preserved his marriage by the aid of Christian patience and regular carnal frolics with Lily, Bless Her.'

'She's been good to him 'as Lily, Bless Her.'

'I must say it's a pleasure to see a woman her age who can still keep up such a splendid front. I suppose, these days, it's mainly a triumph of modern British corsetry but you can't help rejoicing a little at the effect.' Clegg breathed on his glasses and wiped them thoughtfully.

Below them, the car had stopped.

'Sam's going to be sick if he has to give everything up.'

On the warm hillside, amid the hum of insects and the song of the now invisible lark, their thoughts went out to a wounded fellow creature.

'That's old Fairburn's car,' Compo said.

It was too. Fairburn of Co-op Tailoring. Hardly your nature lover. Unimaginative but competent with his measuring tape. Reputed to be a stamp collector. (British Empire and Possessions).

'What the hell's he doing out here with his hand-stitched lapels?'

'It's not really our business,' Foggy said, but continued looking anyway.

'It's nice down there by the river,' Clegg said. 'Poor man's come to rid his lungs of accumulated Harris tweed and flecks of mohair.'

'He can't play bar billiards,' Compo said. 'He made a right balls of it one night in the Eagle.'

'That'll be it then,' Clegg said. 'That's what he's doing down there. Recovering from the humiliation.'

'Give us a fag,' Compo said, 'and stop taking the piss.'

Clegg passed his Players round. 'Maybe he's going to end it all. He could be in there now. Scribbling a final note before he goes in the river.'

'It's not two foot deep.'

'You've no real feeling, have you, for the power of symbolism.'

'Hello, that's her from the bacon counter.' Compo became alert like a trained pointer as the woman and Fairburn left the car. Fairburn was carrying a rug. He looked round nervously before taking the woman's hand. They walked without gaiety into the trees.

'Dirty devil,' Compo said. 'What kind of carry on is that for a stamp collector?'

Clegg turned his back on the scene, depressed by the air of guilt the couple exuded.

'The cheeky sod,' Compo said. 'I wonder if he's getting his divi on that.'

'Will you put your eyes back in your head.' Foggy told him. 'If they fall out altogether they'll roll down the hill and somebody'll have to go and fetch 'em for you. And I'm not picking the damn things up.'

'Can't see a damn thing anyway,' Compo complained. 'All that shrubbery.' He gave up trying and lay back. 'Tell you what. I hope he's slicker than he is at bar billiards.'

Fairburn came out of the trees.

Heavily into his role of guilty Co-op Manager (Tailoring) he chewed his nails on the river bank and looked up at them. The sun glinted from his glasses and made a small moon of his near bald head. He wrapped

11

his arms across his sedentary belly and pressed; bent from the waist, less like a lover than a soul in the grip of powerful gastric emotions.

'You see what new horizons adultery opens up,' Clegg pointed out. 'Instead of being home with his stamps, here he is about to shit himself in the sunshine and fresh air.'

Embarrassed by his embarrassment they made a move to leave but he waved them to wait agitatedly.

As they watched, he performed the tall man's stork dance of removing shoes and socks. His trousers followed and they noted with admiration the training, which even in crisis, prompted Fairburn to fold them neatly before he laid them down.

Then his thin, white legs were entering the water and he was bobbing and weaving at the prick of river-bottom stones and holding up the skirts of his shirt and jacket as he waded across.

He began climbing on tender feet towards them; his Y-fronts unnaturally white.

They could hear his breathing long before he reached them.

He flopped down beside them. 'I thought it were you three,' he gasped. 'Mum's the word then, right?' He began to cough weakly.

They propped him against the wall and undid his neat, managerial collar.

'She's only a slip of a thing,' he said between coughs, 'but we love each other.'

'You great daft sod,' Clegg said.

'She's like a house side,' Compo added.

'She's young,' Fairburn said, playing his trump card.

'Certainly her chin's rather big,' Foggy said.

'Listen!' Fairburn protested weakly, 'I came up here to ask for your discretion, not to get the seal of Good bleeding Housekeeping.'

They gave him a cigarette and made reassuring noises.

'It's not just a physical thing,' he told them. 'It's not that I'm just after humpin' it. It's more spiritual really. The wife's not sympatico. She's got no instinct for frenzy.' He picked reflectively at the sheep shit clogged between his toes. 'These aren't the underpants I normally wear.'

They stared obediently at his gleaming white triangle.

'No, they're longer than these. I've got these baggies. Come nearly down to me knees. They're comfy but that's where me marriage had come to. I popped these on in the shop. I came out here in the car, the sun shining, me heart dancing secure in the knowledge that me underpants were streamlined and clean. I'll have to burn 'em later like. If the wife sees 'em I'm done for. Unless I lock 'em in the cash drawer for next time.' He wiped his glasses on his shirt tail sadly. 'I don't know if I can stand a next time. It starts me guts churnin'. I never expected this sort a thing. I'd no idea she even cared for me till one, magical, slack Thursday when she grabbed me by the nuts in the fitting room.'

Her from the bacon counter came out of the trees.

'Are you bloody coming or aren't you?' she enquired testily. Her voice rang powerfully through the valley.

Fairburn stood up. 'Coming, my love,' he shouted. He turned to them. 'She has eyes,' he said, 'the colour of me favourite green check in the best pattern book. A fourteen ounce thornproof with a faint Lovat fleck.'

They watched him slithering down the hill, his Y-fronts gathering dust.

* * *

They finished their cigarettes and climbed over the wall. They began walking homewards. A rabbit was mashed bloodily in the road.

'Consider the forces,' Clegg said, 'which bring together a rabbit and a vehicle. Or a Tailoring Manager and her from the bacon counter.'

Lily, Bless Her, lived in Sugden Street. There were no flowers in her garden, but at six o'clock that evening they paused on their way to her door to admire certain blossoms on her clothesline. The lingerie of Lily, Bless Her, lacked the high seriousness of the archetypal, local variety.

'It's a picture,' Compo said, his mouth dry, his spirit moved to the verge of incipient poetry.

Cleg was remembering Edith Clegg, deceased. The smell of Mansion Polish – the crackle of static disapproval in the dust-free air – the female garments on the clothes horse; frivolous as lino.

Foggy remembered the Kashmir Gate in Delhi. A blush on the face of the Education Corps sergeant and his own face suffused with blood at the shameless importuning of the two Eurasian whores. Such knickers, he knew from experience, were destructive of an evening's interest in ancient Muslim culture.

The other features of the estate were less noteworthy, consisting of a paved stone yard with additions from a later period in the form of beer cans around the base of a dustbin (municipal circa 1950).

Lily, Bless Her, met them at the door.

Clegg sighed. She was dressed for visiting. Smart navy two-piece and crisp, white, well-filled blouse.

'Now Lily,' Clegg said. 'You know it's no use. You

can't go visiting him. Not while Sybil's there.'

'Law of property,' Foggy said. 'She's got the deeds. Legal wife.'

'In name only,' Lily said.

'She's always done his washing,' Clegg reminded her. 'That counts as powerful medicine round here.'

'I wouldn't mind,' Lily said, 'but she doesn't even like the poor old sod.'

Foggy flinched a little at the directness and felt his Royal Signals tie for comfort. He noticed the paint peeling from the windows. He coughed in embarrassment as he heard Compo saying: 'I like your knickers, Lily.' Nodding towards the line.

'Do you, love?' Lily smiled gratefully. 'Got to keep up appearances. I'm not as young as I used to be.'

But behind her smooth, plump features it was still possible to see the shadow of the girl she had been.

They stood there caps in hand.

'Come in,' she said. 'Don't stand out there. You'll have Her Across needing a hinge in her face. She keeps one eye on her telly and one on me.'

She glowered at a window on the far side of the street. A curtain shivered.

Lily, Bless Her, stood back and held the door open for them. They squeezed past the contours of her hills and valleys. Slowly. Like tourists awed by some great cathedral. She smelled of perfume.

Compo went back for a second trip.

The avenging hand of Foggy dragged him back.

'Gerrof me collar then,' Compo protested as Lily closed the door behind them.

He went to the wall mirror and began indignantly to straighten a tie like a piece of bacon rind. One of his

15

collar points hung limply but more or less in the right direction. The other presented an insubordinate triangle towards the sky. He frowned at it and wet his fingers. He endeavoured to press it back into line, only to see it climb back resolutely. He gave it up.

Foggy shuddered.

'You look like a badly opened envelope,' he complained.

'It's thee,' Compo gave him a sharpish elbow. 'Draggin' folkses' collars about.'

'That piece of grotty linen was mortally wounded before I put me hands on it.'

'It was all right when I left the house.'

'Well which way have you come? Up the Irrawaddy?'

'Go and sit yourselves down,' said Lily, Bless Her. 'I'll get the glasses.'

They stepped over a vacuum cleaner; its flex neglected; ends like pigtails where its plug should be.

They went into the room with her husband on the piano.

He was a hand-coloured lance corporal in a metal frame and battledress before they were worn with ties.

They moved LPs and women's magazines and sat awkwardly down. Three middle-aged men aware of the stare of the eternally youthful corporal. Foggy gorgeous in his blazer with the Royal Signals badge in golden wire. Clegg in the mid-grey suit of former ironmongery days. Compo as if he'd just that moment quit his station in a field deciding 'O to hell with scaring birds.'

A concept of Lily as Yesterday's Honey came potently to Clegg on the traces of her perfume in the room.

Undertones of mould from a cupboard.

The room cool.

A recent picture of her on the fireplace. With handbag

16

and headscarf on some promenade. Her back to the sea. A motherly Russian figure but not a trace of a tractor statistic in that grin. A *babushka* gone wrong. The party's loss – many a comrade's gain.

'I'd have to come back early tonight anyway,' she called over the rinsing of glasses. 'Friday night is Warburton night.'

'Warburton?' Compo asked. 'The Musical Insurance man?'

'The same,' Lily, Bless Her, confessed. 'He comes to me fresh from his triumphs with the Operatic Society.'

'He's a tenor, isn't he?' Foggy enquired.

'Nothing like,' said Lily, Bless Her. 'Wished he was but the market won't stand it round here.'

Foggy shifted in some embarrassment. 'I thought he did *The Mikado*.'

'Not with me,' she said. 'It's a plain Yorkshire menu here. If they want owt exotic they can piss off to Huddersfield. I've no patience wi' folk who think they can't live wi' out blue suspenders.' She appeared outside the door. 'Sam knows,' she said. 'He understands I have a few gentlemen in lieu of any other qualifications.' She went back into the kitchen.

Tins were rattling on a metal tray.

They could hear a kid shouting and the first few bars of *Sound of Music* from the ice cream chimes.

'I hope she 'ant baked any more buns,' whispered Compo.

'I've baked a few more buns,' announced Lily, Bless Her, as she came in with the tray. As well as the glasses and the cans of ale they saw her sinister biscuit tin. It had a picture of St James's Palace on it. Its contents shunted leadenly.

'We'll just have the beer, love,' Compo said, opening

17

his can with the fluid movements of a craftsman.

'Suit yourself. Be more for Sam.'

'Well here's to good old Sam,' said Clegg with feeling. They drank to Sam.

Foggy picked a piece of fluff from his blazer. They looked at St James's Palace.

They sipped their beer.

'I don't know whether he's really ready for 'em,' Clegg said cautiously.

'Rubbish,' snorted Lily, Bless Her. She lifted Bert Kampfert from a cushion and dropped him on the floor. With a rustle of silk she sat down and crossed her knees.

They swallowed more beer.

'O bugger him,' Clegg decided. His eyes on Lily's knees. 'He can have a dip in Old St James's. Take a bit a rough with his smooth.'

'We'll see he gets 'em, Lily,' he said out loud.

What the hell? He survived a thrombosis, didn't he?

'Bless you, love.' She handed him the tin.

He took it in both hands and lowered it carefully to the carpet. The other two were looking at him. He felt like an agent of a foreign power.

'Tell him to shape himself,' said Lily, Bless Her. 'And tell him to write. I've only had one letter.'

She leaned over for her handbag. Foggy, with iron self-control and no little regret, turned his eyes manfully away from the subsequent flash of Lily's limbs. Compo went completely to pieces and fumbled like a novice with his second can.

Lily, Bless Her, rummaged through the bag, discarding gas bills and soap powder vouchers. She found the letter and showed it to them.

'Dear Lily,' it said in a spidery facsimile of Sam's firm

18

hand, 'Did I leave my reading glasses? There's a bloke here knows you from the Three Horse Shoes with a hernia called Trevor. I haven't got to lift but I'm doing nicely, Sam.'

She sniffed.

'That's all I've had. Three weeks now and it's the only news I've had.'

'Give over, love,' said Compo. 'We've been keepin' thee posted.'

Lily waved the letter unconsoled. 'You can tell I must be constantly on his mind. Got the authentic ring of ungovernable passion this has, hasn't it? Just bloody glib is Sam. And who's this bloody Trevor?'

They looked at each other.

'Be him int corner,' Compo said.

'With the screens around?' Foggy said scornfully. 'They don't put screens round a hernia.'

'Me Uncle Dudley had screens round.'

'Agh, yes,' Clegg pointed out. 'But maybe they do put screens round Uncle Dudleys.'

'There's no Trevor in Sam's ward,' Foggy said with the authentic tones of certitude.

'Well you can tell him,' said Lily, Bless Her, 'I don't know no Trevor.'

They got to their feet. Clegg picked up St James's.

'And tell him to get his self out of there. I want a plug on me vac.'

But a canticle of real concern rang plainly in her face.

'Tell him—' she said. 'Tell him. I haven't got his blasted glasses.'

They called in Micklethwaite's for fags.

The bell summoned him from the back, eating a bacon

sandwich. He laid the remains of it on the scales while he wiped his hand on his apron. It weighed nearly three ounces.

'I'll tell thee what,' he said, giving a demonstration of how to talk with your mouth full, loudly. 'Somebody ought to ram summat nasty up the Customs and pissing Excise. V.A.T.!' He pushed back his trilby revealing more hair on his eyebrows than on his head. He splattered a bluebottle with a large tin of herrings.

'That were quick,' Compo said.

'I'm slowing down,' he said ruefully. 'When I were young I could get the bastards wi' a toffee hammer.'

Foggy and Clegg bought Players.

Compo hung back by the detergent shelves, looking underprivileged. 'How's the missis?' he enquired.

'Like a wet fart when it comes to paperwork,' Micklethwaite said.

Outside the street most of the doors were open.

An old man with a white, unshaven face had been brought out on a stool.

Kids were playing on the empty market stalls.

The Carpet Centre was offering Mottled Foam Backed at a pound per yard.

Eichmann went past pushing his barrow with its rich mix of horse dung, chicken shit and pig manure. A tantalizing horticultural blend of his own formula.

'So that's how Sam does it,' Compo leered. 'It's not his sexy eyes then. It's his screwdriver.'

They were on the bus.

The conductor was downstairs, wiping shreds of fluff from Compo's money.

Foggy shared a seat with Clegg. Compo had his wellies on the seat in front.

'Get 'em off,' Foggy ordered.

Compo blew him a kiss. 'Cheeky.'

They took the lid off St James's and peeped at Lily's buns.

They were pale and unnatural.

'Leave 'em on the bus,' Compo said. 'Then after three months they'll belong to whoever handed 'em in.'

'She'll ask him how he enjoyed 'em,' Foggy said. 'He'll have to be able to describe 'em.'

'That's easy enough,' Compo picked one up for a closer examination. 'They look like a bullock's knee-caps.'

Foggy slapped Compo's wrist.

'Stop mauling 'em.'

Clegg put the lid back on.

'She must have followed the recipe,' Foggy said.

'Aye, at a distance.' Clegg put the tin down on an empty seat. 'It's a rare combination; carnality and the catering faculty. I wonder if they ever go together.'

'Our Vera had it,' Compo announced.

'Fairly frequently,' Foggy nodded. 'Even at school.'

'She were top in cookery.'

'I don't know about top,' Foggy continued. 'That time I saw her she was one place under Tommy Haggerty.'

'He married her, din't he?'

'He didn't leave himself a right lot of option, did he?'

'They're happy.'

'I don't now about happy – but I will say with all them kids – at least they're occupied.'

'That's what you get married for, in't it? Kids?'

'Nay not in his case. He'd found out where to get 'em a

21

long time before he got wed.'

Clegg was staring out of the window. 'It's a kind of justice,' he said. 'It's only fair that Lily, Bless Her, should have a feeble catering urge.'

'How come?' Compo enquired, his brow wrinkled with the mild pain of mental effort.

'Cosmic impartiality requires,' explained Clegg, 'that culinary talent should be shared out among those with smaller tits.'

They watched Compo wrestling intellectually with this declaration. He slid his cap a few times round his head; his face twisted, he squashed his nose flat with his hand. After a little while he gave it up and wet his finger and began drawing on the window glass.

'Look at Sybil,' Clegg said.

'Thee look,' Compo protested. 'She were allus snotty even as a lass.'

'I must say,' Foggy looked at Compo pointedly, 'that I sympathize with the urge to improve oneself. A few of us, Sybil included, have dragged ourselves up by the bootheels from inferior social positions.'

'Creeper,' Compo accused.

'It wasn't easy. Swotting there night after night, while he was out climbing Moira Treadgold.'

'I can't help it, Cyril, if tha' din't get thee priorities right.'

'Have less of the Cyril,' Foggy tapped Compo with a stern finger. 'I had my priorities right. At least I finished up with me City and Guilds. What did you finish up with?'

'Spots,' Compo said. 'But it were only measles.'

'How would you describe Sybil?' Clegg asked.

They looked at him. He was still staring out of the

window. A man was walking two Alsatians on a school playing field.

'Very carefully if she were listenin',' Compo said.

The houses on the hillside were new and clean and bright. A young man with his shirt tight over a growing belly was watering his lawn.

'You know where you are with Sybil,' Foggy said.

'You're in the shit,' said Compo. 'Up to here.'

'He must have loved her once.'

'I should think once would be about all he'd get.'

'Why must you vulgarize everything?'

'Because I'm common,' Compo said, and grinned engagingly.

'And repulsive, don't forget,' Clegg prompted.

'And repulsive,' Compo said.

They were entering the city. The pale lights of a supermarket competed feebly with the evening sun.

'Beans are cheap,' Clegg said.

'I'd never have noticed that,' he realized, 'when Edie was alive.'

The man in the store pushing his trolley. Had he been a widower too? It was a grimy area. The only colour was the primary reds of supermarket advertising.

'Epitaph for civilization,' Clegg said. 'Looks like hell but marmalade's down.'

'We used to visit a cousin in this area,' Foggy nodded in the general direction of the side streets. 'Of course it was more respectable then. Trams were still running.' He leaned across Clegg the better to see out of the window. 'They had an aviary. Fascinating really. Up to going there I thought all small birds were brown.'

He settled back in his seat and began to stroke his moustache thoughtfully.

A passenger climbed the stairs and sat down with an evening paper. He had a bulging briefcase and dandruff on his collar. He picked his nose steadily as he read the columns.

From among the holes in his pocket lining, Compo produced his fag tin. He poked about a bit among its rich variety. A cameo of deprivation which would have brought tears of pure marxism to the careers of social workers everywhere. He coughed fruitily in case the others had failed to notice.

'Who's that scruffy gentleman poking about in that fag tin?' Clegg said, picking up his cue like a professional.

'Don't look!' Foggy instructed. 'Sometimes they go away.'

'Can it be true,' Clegg enquired, 'that he hasn't got a whole cigarette among that entire collection?'

'Soddin' can,' Compo said showing him the evidence. 'And after I gave me blood for me country an' all.'

'Isn't that appalling?' Clegg said, probing through the tin's contents with an inquisitive finger. 'Not one. Tell you what I'll do.'

'What then?' Compo enquired.

'I'll take this one,' Clegg said, pulling out one of the fatter specimens.

'Tha's got no soul,' Compo glared, grabbing the tin, and slamming it firmly shut.

'I wouldn't touch that,' Foggy advised as he watched Clegg prepare to light it. 'Not if they paid me. It'll be seething with vile green bacteria.'

'It's true,' Compo said.

'It's an age of tolerance,' Clegg smiled with a patent charity. 'What's all this prejudice against vile green bacteria?'

24

They watched him light it. Foggy for signs of rigor mortis: Compo as a child might watch his rabbit being fondled by a cook.

'Me best bloody tab,' he said.

'Aw!' said Clegg.

'I were keepin' that till I got in bed tonight,' Compo protested. 'I have a can of ale and a last drag an' I'm away like a light.'

Clegg passed the tab to Foggy. 'Hold this a minute.'

Foggy accepted it gingerly, and held it at arm's length, waiting for it to bite.

Clegg reached over and pinned Compo to his seat. He began to tickle him. Compo kicked and threshed violently: yawping and laughing helplessly.

'Show us your inside pocket!' Clegg demanded.

'It's empty,' Compo shrieked as Clegg dug his fingers in his ribs again. He lay on his back now, writhing with laughter.

Foggy tried to look like a comparative stranger.

The man with the evening paper pretended nothing was happening. He turned a page.

'Look at him,' Compo yelled. 'I'm being mugged, mister, and you're readin' the bloody paper.'

'It's not a mugging, mister,' Clegg said. 'It's just that we can't afford to keep him. His licence has expired.'

He renewed the attack on the almost helpless Compo who made signs of surrender. Clegg, poised for the attack again, allowed him to sit up. Compo reached inside his pocket. Slowly he brought out an almost new packet of Players.

'Well, I'll go to hell,' he said, grinning shamelessly. 'If thy hadn't made me look, I might have forgotten all about them.'

The conductor was at the top of the stairs looking for the source of the noise.

Compo switched his grin into an expression of sheer agony and began writhing in simulated pain on his seat.

'What's up wi' him?' the conductor asked, approaching cautiously.

Clegg caught his toe on Lily's bun tin. 'St James's disease,' he said. He stroked Compo's brow. Compo took the opportunity to bite him.

The conductor flinched. 'He'll have to get off if he's violent,' he said.

Compo rolled his eyes.

'We're getting off at the infirmary,' Clegg explained.

'Will he be sick?' asked the conductor doubtfully.

'Well I can't guarantee it,' Clegg said. 'But if you like I could ask him.'

'They've been fooling about,' said the man with the paper. 'Like kids they are.'

'It may have looked like that,' Clegg admitted. 'But would you believe Artificial Respiration?'

'The kiss of life?' The conductor was becoming increasingly suspicious.

'Nay bugger that,' Clegg said. 'There's a limit to everything.'

'Fooling about!' the man with the paper said.

'With a bit more effort,' Clegg said, pointing to the man with the paper, 'I bet you could become one of nature's real shitpots.'

They were thrown off two stops before the infirmary.

A last minute attempt to placate the conductor with a bun having proved totally ineffectual.

Sam looked grey. He wore his headphones in bed but they were switched off, which is more than could be said for Sybil who complained steadily while she knitted and kept a critical eye on the other visitors to the ward.

He could barely hear it and he had in reserve great earfuls of music at the twist of a knob. It was like watching her from a place of concealment.

Her complexion was still good. Between the crows' feet the skin was a smooth wax fruit. Light pine maybe under a clear varnish. The kind of sheen some petals have. He thought of cactus blooms. That one brief flower and the rest is thorns.

No make-up. The face had renounced cosmetics and laughter. For both of which there were good biblical authorities, Sam realized, but sod it anyway. Those crows' feet marked the passing of the flocks of gloom. A few laugh lines would have been better. O Lord, give her the grace to see how lumpen is that chapel hat!

She was always handsome.

A kind of Spanish face.

The hair become the colour of steel.

Lord?

Are you listening?

Is anybody there?

Then who coagulates these pellets causing havoc in my blood?

We are resisting you with chemicals. But for how long? I shall escape to go home this time but what then?

And how appalling anyway if May and Baker were to win. I have to die to consolidate your authority. But you might as well know that it will always be a barrier between us that Sybil, in her middle years, developed hairs on her shins.

I reckon being dead has got to be easy.

Some of the biggest twats I've ever known have been doing it for years: successfully. It's the dying, isn't it?

That bloke in the corner in Intensive Care had a struggle. Involving much activity for the night shift.

But afterwards was quiet.

No strain.

No fuss.

He let them wheel him quietly out to the mortuary, leaving the contents of his locker top untouched.

He never even came back for his orange juice: not while I was there.

Nobody's died in here yet.

He looked round the ward.

Cosgrave's wife has decent knees. She was leaning forward in her chair alongside Cosgrave's bed – her skirt slipping up.

She never takes her eyes off him.

She squeezes his hand whenever she can.

He lets her when he thinks nobody's looking. She's forty-five and badly dressed and lovely.

She brings him books and massive quantities of affection. It does him more good than his medication. She'll have him home in no time.

Sam looked down at his own hand against the whiteness of the sheet. It was becoming old. The pallor of sickness didn't suit it. He noted the liver spots and the corrugations. It was missing the leathery dignity of occupation.

A bit of sun wouldn't hurt it.

He stared through the double glazing of the sealed windows. The sky above the operating theatre was a travel brochure blue. A small, white cloud as clean as matron, slipped out of sight behind A-block.

'That Cosgrave's wife,' Sybil frowned, 'wants to learn how to sit properly.'

'She idolizes him,' Sam said, taking off his phones. 'That is sitting properly.'

'I might have known you'd think so.'

Sam's spirits rallied as he heard them coming: the posher public tones of Foggy chiding Compo for some breach of deportment. Sybil stiffened. They advanced grinning. Sam flinched momentarily at the sight of the advancing bun tin. He glanced at Sybil. Her antennae were already waving about it suspiciously.

'Who baked them then?' she enquired.

'He did.' They said in perfect unison, each pointing at each other.

Sam closed his eyes in pain.

'It were joint,' Compo explained. 'We all did a bit. We like your hat. Don't we like her hat?'

'Ravishing as ever,' Clegg said, 'and that's only Sam.' He gave Sam a playful thump. 'How are you then?'

'He dun't look well,' Compo volunteered, peering closer.

They settled in. Each very conscious of Sybil. There was a strained silence.

'They only like two to a bed,' she informed them.

'Don't we all?' Compo said. Foggy dug him quickly in

29

the ribs. 'Hey up!' Compo protested. 'Pack it in. Why is it every time we go anywhere I finish up wi' bruised ribs?'

'You wouldn't want us to mark your face would you?' Clegg asked.

'Not only that,' Foggy added with feeling. 'We wouldn't even like to handle it.

'I just wondered,' Compo said.

The silence this time seemed to be centred around the bun tin. It lay on Sam's locker-top, quietly dominating the proceedings.

'What's tha' knittin', Sybil?'

'Nothing you need to know about.'

Clegg watched her for a moment.

'I bet you had more fun round the guillotine.'

Sam grinned. Sybil counted her stitches.

'He's not supposed to have food brought in,' she said.

'Just a gesture,' Clegg said. 'We'll take it back again.'

'Seems funny bringing it then,' Sybil accused. She put down her knitting and reached for the tin. They watched her nervously.

'Lid sticks,' Compo said.

'It's coming.' Sybil said patiently.

'Me best tin,' Compo charged. 'Go steady with it.'

It was hidden from him as she bent over it.

'What's it a picture of?' she asked. She fastened the others with a knowing glare before they could prompt him.

They turned their attention to Compo.

He was twisting his hat round his head again.

'Me mam went in hospital when they did her appendix,' he said.

'Never mind your mam's appendix,' Sybil ordered. 'Tell us what the picture is. On your tin.'

'Buckingham Palace.'

Sybil showed the tin with an air of triumph.

'Is what they usually are,' Compo continued, 'but this one in't, this one's St James's.'

'I'll take him out a minute,' Foggy said. 'There's only supposed to be two round a bed.' He hauled Compo into the corridor. Compo waved briefly before he was yanked out of sight, protesting.

Sybil had the lid off now and was staring at the contents. She looked up quizzically at Clegg.

'Let it be acknowledged, Sybil, that you have superior buns,' Clegg admitted.

Sybil lifted a specimen into the light and showed it to her husband.

'All these years I've been singing "Rock of Ages",' she said. 'It's the first time anybody's ever come up with a piece.'

'Not enough fat that's all,' Sam said.

'There's fat enough where this came from,' Sybil said in tones which brooked no argument.

She dropped the bun back in the tin with a meaningful thud.

'It's all irrelevant,' Sam sighed, 'seeing as I'm going to be dead.'

'You can't evade your responsibilities like that,' she said.

'It's a bloody good start,' he said, looking at Clegg for support.

'He means it,' Sybil informed Clegg.

'Nay give over,' Clegg protested. 'He'll be home next week.'

'Aye and when I get out they'll not get me back in,' Sam insisted. 'They're all right. They're good enough.

But it's not home, is it?'

Sybil looked at her husband. 'Since when have you ever known where your home is?'

'I've always known.' He returned her stare. 'I never liked it much but I've always known.' He turned to Clegg. 'I've been wanting to get you two on your own. I want a word. You're a witness, Clegg. I want our Colin to have me lathe and me woodturning tools.'

'That's right,' Clegg said. 'Put a good face on it.'

Sam ignored him and looked at Sybil enquiringly.

'Shall I send me suit to Oxfam?'

'O I should,' Clegg said. 'I can just see some little brown bugger running round a palm tree in a blue serge ensemble.'

'All right. Let your mate have it.'

'Compo?'

'Why not?'

'All right. In about twenty years when you've finished with it.'

'He'll get it afore then.'

'Well I hope he can steer it,' Sybil said. 'Else it'll keep dragging him round to her in Sugden Street.'

She picked up her knitting again and the needles began to fly rapidly.

Clegg shifted uncomfortably.

'What about me watch?' Sam asked.

'Do what you like with it,' Sybil said.

'It were me grandad's,' he explained. He looked at Sybil. 'It'll be worth a bit.'

'Please yourself what you do with it.' She sounded as if she meant it. 'I don't want it.'

'Might as well go to our Colin then,' Sam said.

'He will think it's Christmas,' Sybil sniffed haughtily.

'My brother the Oil Sheik.'

'Is that how it's going to look?' Sam asked, looking worried now. 'Will they think I'm showing off?'

'Bound to,' Clegg said, fed up with the whole proceeding. 'There goes our kid he'll say. Showing off 'cos he's dead.'

'Well bugger me,' Sam complained. 'When you get down to it – nothing's easy is it?'

He looked at Sybil. 'You'd best keep it then.'

'I don't want it.'

'Do as you're told, woman. Keep it.' He turned to Clegg. 'You're a witness. See she keeps it.'

'Tell you what,' Clegg said. 'Why don't you hang about and keep the bloody thing yourself?'

'You don't have to go that far,' Sybil added. 'If that's the alternative I'll keep it.'

They watched her bent over her knitting. She let their silence last for a long moment and then turned on them.

'Shocked are you? Am I supposed to weep because he's mooning on about being dead? Look at him. Got monk on now because nobody with a violin's turned up. Well it's too late, son, for me to start feeling sorry for you. I can't see that thrombosis has done all that much to revolutionize your character. You'll see. Once he gets back on his feet he'll be as foul as ever.'

Sam looked at her. 'You're a hard bugger, Sybil,' he told her with a quiet pride.

'Are you sure you want to go home?' Clegg enquired. 'Wouldn't you rather stay here and have an operation or summat?'

'She'll nurse me if she has to,' Sam pointed out. 'It won't be gentle mebbe, but she'll do her duty.'

Clegg felt relief when the bell went.

He took the bun tin, gave Sam a friendly thump and legged it to the door.

He waited for Sybil in the corridor.

'He wants cheering up,' he told her.

She met his eyes steadily.

'Then he mun go where he gets his buns,' she said. 'She's the one thinks life is summat to laugh about.'

He watched her walking to the lift; her sensible shoes tapping firmly on the tiled floor.

He found Compo in Maternity trying to plead guilty by association as he stood next to a row of cots.

Foggy was in the main entrance area, arguing nationalization heatedly with a porter.

They went into the park and threw buns at the ducks.

'Birds with more spirit,' Clegg suggested, 'would be throwing 'em back.'

'That bloody porter,' Foggy said, 'is going round preaching like a Muscovite and all on the National Health.'

'He were all right were Joe Stalin,' Comp said.

Foggy took the bait better than the ducks and they were off. Clegg listened for a while to their arguments. He stared at the setting sun. Midges were loping crazily above the water. The sky was like an open furnace door. As red as a clot in a critical artery, Clegg thought. Are they red? Or is it dark, satanic plum? He shook the crumbs out of the bun tin into the water and they sank like pellets. Some dull, drab mallard Sybil gave him a beady look.

'And you!' he told her in answer to her peevish quack.

It was dusk when they got to the Three Legs. They found Lily, Bless Her, in the best room drinking Guinness. Mister Warburton, the insurance man, was patting her knee sympathetically and doing rapid calculations regarding his interest. Some of the springtime fled from his smile when he discovered Compo grinning at him.

'Hey up then Warburton,' Compo said. 'Get 'em in.'

And under the eyes of Lily, Bless Her, what could he do but oblige?

He went to the bar expansively opening his purse a crack or two.

'How's Sam then?' enquired Lily, Bless Her.

'Be home soon,' Clegg said. 'Sends his ta for the buns.'

Night lay on the town like too many blankets. Like the gas capes in Burma, Foggy remembered. The ones you sweated under. They kept the rain out but it really didn't matter.

He kicked off the last sheet and listened to his landlady's clock chiming every quarter.

At two thirty he switched on the light. His cigarettes were arranged neatly with his matches on the dresser. He lit one. He sat up in bed to smoke it.

At this hour, the young soldier in the frame near his hairbrush was more remote and unbelievable than any stranger. A pink young Foggy.

He became oppressed suddenly by the weight of the realization of how irreversible was the distance between him and the young man in the photo.

He pulled open a drawer and from underneath his shirts took out his box. He laid his medals out in regulation order across his pillow. But even these, tonight, had not what memory required of them. New elements in his perception kept insisting upon their banality. As it did, these days, for enemies whose cars were now seen daily in the streets.

He smoked carefully. Using the lid of his Nivea cream for an ash tray. In this way he stood sentry, waiting, for the relief of morning: for the blessed trivia of day.

Compo in his smoke grey, midnight, diabolicals of ghostly underwear, flushed his outside toilet and paddled barefoot painfully across the surface of the yardway, back into the house.

The ferrets were rearing in their cages. The odours of uncertainty strong about them; the unshaded bulb making them angry with its glare.

He spoke to them softly. Soothing them while he picked the cinders from his feet. He put the light out and crooned to them further. He could sense them moving. Quieter now. Calmer. Like reeds in a clear stream.

The tap was dripping in the old glazed stone sink. He kicked the door wider open for a breath of air. Some of the roofs of the town were below him.

. How many rooms, he wondered, with a pair in? Somebody to talk to when you can't sleep.

'You remember Muriel,' he said to the ferrets. 'That Mew. Cleared off wi' me wireless,' he told them, jogging areas of furry cortex, 'an' all them brass handles off me wardrobe.'

Crafty bitch. I never knew they were worth owt, else I'd have had 'em first. Just shows. Tha lives an' learns.

Not just a bit of umpty but an education.

'I'd have her back though,' he confessed to the ferrets. 'Not just 'cos there's nowt else to nick either.'

He hadn't got his hat on to twist so he pushed his face about in the struggle to frame the warmth of his recollection of Mew.

'Half way pissed,' he told them. 'There was nobody nicer.'

He kept an emergency can of ale for just such moments of nostalgia, in the old copper in the wash house. But of course he'd drunk it. So he rattled about a bit in the dark, with the aid of matches, for his ferrets' sake so he could later toast Muriel in a mug of scalding tea that made him sweat. Light-fingered bitch. Wherever she might be.

'Doing bloody porridge I shouldn't wonder.'

He made some bread and milk up for the ferrets.

'Get this inside thee,' he ordered. 'Might as well all have a soddin' picnic. Milk's going off anyway.'

He listened to the small sounds of their lapping between sups of his tea.

'I'll tell thee what Mew,' he announced to the humid night air. 'They're daintier bloody eaters than thee.'

Cleg was reading.

Edie had never sanctioned reading in bed. Insomnia, formerly, had had to be suffered.

The Methodist ethic?

Clegg wiped the sweat from his forehead and realized he was still more or less in his own side, his old side, of the marital bed.

Marital bed?

I suppose it must have been. But with all the enormous decorum of a middle-aged couple, in full weatherproofs, on the back of a motor cycle.

He looked at the unmarked pillow by his side. The lack of imprint on the familiar space somehow more powerful than any indentation.

Mark of the eternal absence of his mate.

I shall never get over the strangeness.

Edie gone.

We were never close. But always together and that finally becomes more powerful than close. It can leave your heart untouched, your arguments unresolved, but fashion somehow a kind of one flesh.

Osmosis.

The true mysteriousness of marriage. Overcoming

discord, unlikeness, antipathy. Feeding on them even as the rich loam of its achievement.

It was a night for lightness and he was trying hard to follow a sub-standard Marlow through brittle pastures of downtown LA. But it was no go. The unreality was massive.

Some of these shamuses should anyway make Clegg-like with the broads and find sashaying through their office doors a client or two like Edie.

That'll hold 'em for a while.

'Cept Edie's school plays trouble clamlike to its own breast. Wouldn't be seen dead, let me tell you, revealing details of the family feuds to some wise arse with a bottle in his drawer, never mind swinging one long, nyloned, tantalizing smooth expanse of leg across the other under his nose. I promise you.

Christ! She had stockings you couldn't see to rob a bank through.

And anyway Edie's right. The times are overburdened with confession anyway.

Come back reticence – all is forgiven.

Scent she never wore but kept from Christmases and birthdays, was on the dresser. He reached over and unstoppered one, sniffing, thinking – this was Edie had she worn it – but she didn't and it wasn't.

The house was Edie.

He kept it as near as he could how she liked it. Apart from his clothes strewn on the chair. He began to fold them tidily. A small agnostic offering.

To what?

He didn't know as he pottered about in their bedroom at three o'clock in the morning.

All he knew was that Edie had been beeswax and rectitude and Windolene.

Sybil lies sleeping in the sunless cool of the spare bedroom – where milk weeps coolest – where Sam has slept these many years. Her feet not far from his boots in the wardrobe. Intimacy by their standards.

And in Sugden Street, uncorseted soft overspill of Lily, Bless Her, heaving slightly – tidal – as she snores. In her advancing path, a chastened Warburton – the spend-thrift moment gone – abandons the last damp slice of undigested bed. Performs deft morning movements with his braces. A sly matins of a furtive dressing. Then downstairs, prudentially, with Co-op shoes in hand.

Sam listens to the night nurse making tea.
    She finds him smoking and brings him a cup.
    She is an ugly, pleasant girl.
    He watches her walking back to her cubicle in the dim institutional light.
    Angel of mercy.
    Arse like a brewer's dray.
    If I had my time over, he tell himself, I'd cultivate nothing but her sort.
    All bonny in their own way.
    It requires more refinement of taste to appreciate it, that's all.
    A wiser palate, sod it, comes too late.
    Just as exciting are those of odd shape.
    And vastly more gentle of character.
    Would there be time, he wondered, for an ageing, ailing man to affect a surreptitious snatch when she passes?
    Nothing too radical, he promised his fluttering heart.
    And only when I'm feeling a bit better of course.

40

The day of Sam's homecoming. Cloudy but warm. They called on Sybil at the bungalow.

Good Estate Agents' country. The neat, small dwellings changing hands with frequency.

But Sybil's at the more solid end. The little garden matured. Rugged Sam craftsmanship in garden woodwork. Rebellious Sam gamesmanship in the rough planking of his sod-the-neighbours shed.

Sybil wiping already spotless paintwork on a stool in down-at-heel shoes and an old summer dress. Her unsupported breasts blending with the rest of her. Shapeless floral tube.

'O God – those giddy, mad years of the menopause,' Clegg thought as he watched her from the gate.

She stretched and they saw the tops of her stockings like idiot, slack smiles, sagging from the white faces of her legs.

Clegg turned his back. Depressed.

Remembered Edie, on honeymoon, rubbing Vick on her chest.

Behind his back, of course, naturally.

Foggy averted his eyes and slid Compo's cap down as far as his nose.

Sybil climbed down from the stool and regarded them suspiciously.

'Is he home then yet?' Compo enquired.

'No. And he won't be for hours yet.'

'Where is he then?' Clegg asked.

'They've an ambulance coming this way about tea time. They'll bring him on that.'

'I thought he could come home this morning,' Clegg looked at Foggy's watch. It was nearly eleven o'clock.

'If he had his own transport,' Sybil said.

'Taxi,' Clegg said.

She looked at him steadily. 'We haven't got daft money like that.'

'Looking very bonny, your delphiniums,' Foggy complimented her; raising his hat.

'Creeper,' Compo looked at him with disgust.

'They want weeding,' Sybil stated flatly.

'Have you got his bed ready if we fetch him earlier?' Clegg asked.

The others looked at him in some surprise.

'There's no coloured fairy lights on it if that's what you mean,' Sybil told him. 'It doesn't say "Welcome Home Sam" in red, white and blue paper. But it's aired. It's clean.'

She picked up the stool and walked with it to the back door.

She turned and sought Clegg's eyes.

'You'd better make sure first where he wants to come. Here or Sugden Street.'

She wiped the sweat from her brow with the back of her hand. Blew a strand of hair back from her face.

'If he doesn't know his self. Ask him how poorly he feels. If he feels bad enough he'll want bringing here.'

She went indoors.

'She's right tha knows,' Compo nodded. 'If he's feeling miserable his thoughts are bound to turn to Sybil.'

He dug Foggy smartly in the ribs. Laid his head coyly on his shoulder. Looked up in his eyes.

'Tha' never says owt delicious about my delphiniums.'

Foggy brushed him away in horror.

'Get away. I'd sooner have a lavatory seat round me neck. Keep your distance. Walk behind, can't you? It's a respectable area. It does me no good to be seen with the likes of you. Go lie down under a car. It's the only part you've ever been properly dressed for.'

Foggy set off in pursuit of Clegg. Compo tagged on undeflated.

'Where are we off to?' Foggy caught up with Clegg. 'How are we going to get Sam home?'

'Borrow Sid's van.' Clegg sounded as if the idea was reasonable.

'A fish and chip van?' Foggy stared incredulously.

'About the same size as an ambulance,' Clegg pointed out. 'Bags a room.'

'He'll be able to catch up on his newspapers,' Compo said, slipping his arm matily through Foggy's.

'If you don't move off,' Foggy said, 'I shall employ somebody who specializes in these matters – to piss down your welly.'

'Can you drive it?' Sid looked at Clegg doubtfully.

'I'm not a mechanical cretin,' Clegg protested.

'No,' Sid admitted. 'But you're bloody close.'

It was parked on Corporation waste ground. Cinders, where the fairs came. Where the river ran through the town.

It was bigger than Clegg remembered.

Sid tossed him the keys.

With a sense of impending farce, Clegg climbed into the cab.

43

Good visibility.

I'm going to be able to see whatever I hit.

He looked at the vast space behind and around him.

What a bloody performance just for a few chips.

It smelled of fat.

He twiddled the gear lever.

I suppose it is the gear lever. Not some diabolical selector for the size of his chips.

I'm going to look a right prune trying to change gear with his bleedin' taty peeler.

Between the disused mill and the chimney, the piece of non-corporation sky was blue and friendly.

Vast banks of frothy cumulus just right for hitting with a damn great van.

But look what I've got down here!

Gritstone walls, that's all.

Sodding great mill folk have finished with and just left.

And left it where?

Right in the path of Sid's rotten van.

Going to need some fancy juggling to get it out of here.

He slid open the driver's window and smiled sheepishly at Sid.

'Did you have to leave it pointing straight at the bloody river?'

Sid sighed. He climbed up into the cab and turned the van round. He switched off again and handed back over to Clegg.

'We'll wait out here with Sid,' Compo said. 'Till you get the feel of it.'

Cheeky sod.

Freaking out already.

He started the engine at the third attempt. Buzzed the

throttle, a bit, professionally. Then grated everybody's teeth for a mile trying to grind it into gear.

'There's no synchromesh,' Sid was trying to bellow over the noise of a racing clutch. 'Not on first gear.'

'There isn't now,' Foggy said.

They watched, fascinated, as the van began a series of lunges across the cinders, like a foot playing hopscotch.

'The handbrake,' Sid was yelling. 'Free the handbrake.'

In the silence of the stall which followed, sparrows could be heard chattering inside the battered mill windows.

Clegg hit the starter again.

Four, long, whining chords before the van again began its series of lurches as if it were being repeatedly goosed.

In the silence of the second stalling there carried – along with the sounds of the river in its liquid passing over stones; over cans; over the axles of a pram – the noises of Sid crying, 'O no! O shit!' repeatedly to the elderberries on the bank as he turned his face away from the convulsions of the van.

'Trouble with Sid is,' Clegg signalled a bicycle to over-take, 'he thinks he's the only bugger can drive this thing.'

They had left the town behind. In the euphoria which comes with hedgerows, meadows and the open road, Clegg was contemplating a daring sortie into third gear.

But then there were the hills.

He decided to leave well enough alone for the time being.

Foggy sat with his feet spread between empty crisp containers.

God! How the mighty are fallen.

It's a good job me mother's dead.

Especially when you consider that we buried her.

He chastized himself with a sense of guilt for the wayward thought.

Permitting funnies about his mother. God rest her.

Something insidious happening to his moral fibre.

Beginning to think the same way as these two lunatics he's keeping company with.

Right pair of Herberts.

He stared out through the fatty fingermarks on the window.

What am I – scion of the house of Foggy – which me mother kept like a little palace – student of the pianoforte – earmarked for a life of quiet service behind the throne with the Water Board – if the war hadn't intervened – retired Warrant Officer Royal Signals – doing here in a second-hand chip van – painted mauve for Christ's sake – being driven at this reckless walking pace by a redundant lino salesman from the Co-op – with delusions of mechanical aptitude and a bloody silly flat hat on?

He noted Clegg's death grip on the wheel. The terrible intensity of his expression.

And as for the other bugger!

Obscene Oswald poking about in the back somewhere. Peering into the fry pans and nosing into the storage cupboard under the serving counter.

He glared at Compo, 'You will make yourself at home, won't you?'

'It's full of owd spuds under here,' Compo reported. ''Alf on 'em wi' sprouts on.'

There's really nobody in my circle, Foggy decided.

Anybody of any real substance in town is either dead,

moved to Harrogate, else working.

If I want company during the day this is it.

He sneaked covert glances at his two companions.

What a choice.

Loneliness or lunacy.

'There int arf some clag under here,' Compo announced, his head in the storage cupboard, his arse exposed. 'Bits of owd chips. All sorts.'

'Isn't it marvellous?' Foggy flinched at the indelicate vision of Compo's rear. 'You leave him two minutes in a strange place and he flies unerringly to where it's grimiest like a homing pigeon.'

'It's still a source of controversy among scientists,' Clegg announced, closing his eyes momentarily as a bus passed, 'but then what isn't?'

'What is?' Foggy asked.

'I've forgotten,' Clegg said. 'Shurrup, I'm trying to concentrate.'

They drove in silence for half a mile. On the horizon westwards thunderclouds were building.

'Homing pigeons,' Clegg volunteered. 'That was it. That's what I was on about. Bird migratory faculties generally. Tell you what. They get where they want to go a damn sight less long windedly than scientists.'

'Or chip vans,' Foggy added.

'They reckon they've got a built-in compass.'

'I used to have a pair of fantails,' Compo informed them.

'You should wear 'em whatever it is,' Foggy told him. 'Cover up that raggy britches arse.'

'They're pigeons,' Compo said scornfully. 'They were a lovely pair.'

He stretched out comfortably on the serving counter.

47

'I think next door's cat must a got 'em.'

'Are you sure it's not a panther?' Foggy enquired, "cos you look as if you've been mauled a few times.'

Clegg chuckled and blew the horn.

'I've been wondering what that bugger was,' he admitted.

The smile left his face as they came to the brow of the hill and began the descent into the city.

It was fine as far as the zebra.

The city fathers, in their wisdom, had decreed that the crossing outside the shopping precinct should be uncontrolled.

The crowds came out of the precinct and swarmed across to the shops on the other side of the road.

They were like extras being chivvied out of the bar for the revolutionary scene. Which come to think of it is not unlike the revolutionary scene.

The city drivers knew the drill for getting through.

The accepted rule was to inch your bumper forward until it hung above one or other of the black or white rectangles. In this position, the driver was considered to be in play.

Alert pedestrians, actually on the crossing at this time, and those fast enough off the kerb to follow through, could continue going across providing they slapped the vehicle bonnet smartly while uttering the I-intend-to-cross-your-path-now signal.

This consisted of the words, 'get back you bastard' delivered while in motion and accompanied by one of several approved gestures.

The appearance on the crossing, of the first, nervous elderly lady, on the other hand marked the crucial tactical point of the game. Should she hesitate, the

48

advantage was understood to have passed to the driver, who was then expected to complete his move.

Clegg, of course, had no chance.

Perspiring freely, he waited, in his innocence, for a van-sized space.

For seven and half minutes by Foggy's watch, which unlike Foggy was not prone to exaggeration.

The mile of vehicles behind him were becoming restless. Their flashing lights and sounding horns were saying things that the corporation would have had to remove had they been written on walls.

A few drivers in his immediate rear had left their vehicles and attempted to interfere with the pedestrian flow. But roughly handled, under rule 3B had quickly returned to their cabs, tucking their shirt flaps in and straightening their ties.

'Bloody hippies,' Clegg said. 'You know what they'd do. Abandon everything and swan off into the waiting caves of C & A.' He looking longingly upon the entrance to the store.

The referee arrived in the shape of an elderly policeman. In summer shirt sleeves, a transmitter in the pocket over his bulging chest, he ran his eyes cynically over Sid's hand-painted panels. He leaned through the cab window towards Clegg, his idiot detector registering 'maximum', and said in tones of utter reasonableness.

'Why don't you do us all a favour – and take your portable, purple pisshouse somewhere else?'

He held back the pedestrian flow. 'Now,' he said, when the crossing was completely clear, 'do you think you could hit that?'

Clegg drove past the competent, seen-it-all eyes, his face crimson.

'It's mauve,' Foggy said, when they were safely past. 'He shouldn't be allowed to talk like that.'

'Remind me,' Clegg said, 'to come back another way.'

Sam was dressed and waiting in the Recreation Room. He was watching the under-fives programme with a rubber-faced pensioner with no teeth. This one was in a hospital dressing gown. Pint sized. Somebody's ga-ga doll of a grandad, Sam decided.

A sixteen-year-old nurse came in and tidied the old man's hair. 'Have you had your cocoa, Mister Paisley?' she enquired in loud, good-natured, kindergarten tones.

But she was blocking his view and the old man plucked her peevishly out of his way.

She smiled at Sam, gave a final pat to the old man's hair and left.

'In't there owt else on?' Sam hinted.

'Ahm watching this,' Mr Paisley said firmly.

'All right,' Sam said. 'I'll be patient with you. On account of you being a bit of a stupid old pillock.'

'Arseholes!' said Mr Paisley.

'It's the positive side of institutional life,' Sam declared, 'this opportunity for striking up new relationships.' He looked at the old man who was following the activities of a wooden puppet with rapt attention.

Sam walked over to the automatic dispenser. 'Do you want a shandy?' he enquired.

'I can't pay nowt for it.' The old man looked at him with crafty eyes.

'That's sad. And I suppose you're too proud to accept charity.'

'Don't shek it about,' said Mr Paisley.

'Are you ready?' Clegg asked, grinning around the door.

'I'd a been ready Wednesday,' Sam said, 'but I had a little grab at a night nurse and it put me blood pressure up. Set me back two days.' He sighed. 'I'm right out a condition.'

'Come on home. We'll get you back into it,' Clegg said.

'Shut that door,' said Mr Paisley.

Sam had his few things in a carrier bag. As they rode down with him in the lift he tabulated his future.

'No cream cakes, no animal fats, no fornication.'

'It's time you packed it in anyway,' Clegg grinned. 'Cream cakes at your age. Disgusting.'

They walked him steadily to the van.

He stared at it.

'Christ!' he exclaimed. 'No expense spared.'

'You didn't want to wait in there any longer, did you?' Foggy asked.

'No,' admitted Sam, thinking of the under fives and Mister Paisley.

'In my wallet,' Foggy said with the air of a successful conjuror, 'is a folded triangle of faded silk which will lend this expedition a touch of style. The old red, white and blue.' He produced a small pennant. 'This little emblem accompanied me the length and breadth of Burma.'

'Anybody normal had french letters,' Compo said disgustedly.

'On my wireless jeep. It's been through shot, shell and prickly heat. We'll fly it now to indicate a VIP aboard.' He began fastening it to Sid's corroded aerial. He stepped back to admire it. It hung limply.

'It looks just like I feel,' Sam said.

'She'll fly bravely enough when we get under way,' Foggy promised.

'Listen,' Clegg said, 'I'm not tearing through town just to flutter your laundry.'

'It needs only a little wind,' Foggy explained patiently.

Compo raised a leg obligingly and the crackle of a fart echoed among the parked vehicles. They scattered.

'Oo, it's great to be alive,' Sam said, wrinkling his nose cautiously.

They helped him into the van.

Compo smiled encouragingly. 'Tha wunt a got that in an ambulance,' he said. 'That dun't get the individual touch.'

Foggy pointed firmly. 'Get in the back.'

And on the way home she did fly bravely. Sam regarded the fluttering triangle through the windscreen. Behind it the hills and the trees filled him with a sense of beauty and regret. He saw the town of his birth in the crotch of the valley. Its churches. Its mill chimneys.

'Bonny day,' he said.

'It'll rain later,' Foggy said, pointing to the gathering dark cumulus in the west.

Sam pulled on his forbidden cigarette. There is that, he decided. It'll be better being dead when it's pissing down. No it won't. Can't be bad in winter though. O God I'm going to miss the spring.

It came to him urgently like a fist plucking his bowels. He grabbed Clegg's arm.

'Hey up! Stop! What about me ashes?'

Clegg swerved and hit the brakes.

'Flick 'em on the floor for Christ's sake.' He looked at Sam indignantly.

'My ashes,' Sam said. 'When I've snuffed it.'

'We're all going to snuff it,' Compo complained as he

picked himself and Foggy up from the floor, 'if tha's going to carry on like that.'

'You're only saying that,' Sam challenged. 'When it comes to the crunch, I bet I have to go on me own.'

'We'll write,' Foggy said huffily, flicking the odd chip from his garments. 'Just send us your address.'

'It's right here,' Sam pointed through the window. 'This is it.' His fingers dug into Clegg's arm. 'I want to hear you promise. All of you. Now. That you'll scatter 'em round here.' He checked each in turn for their confirmation. He settled back in his seat and relaxed. 'Somewhere where they're not likely to build. I don't want 'em going straight though me with a bleedin' motorway. It's nice up here. I can see Duckett's foundry and Mottishaw's bakery. I shall know where I am.'

'Here he is,' Clegg called as he rang Sybil's doorbell. They propped Sam in the open doorway. 'He's home.'

'Take his boots off then,' Sybil shouted from somewhere inside, 'I'm not having him tramping on my carpets. His boots aren't poorly. They can still rough up me twisted Wilton.'

'Listen,' Sam grabbed Clegg's arm. 'Come and get me when she's gone to bed. Sneak me down to Lily's.'

'You're not ready for Lily,' Clegg said. 'You'll have to get back in training first. Start with something easy. Build yourself a garage.'

The appearance of Sybil put a stop to the discussion.

'I don't know what that damn thing is you've left parked in the street but you can shift it; quick as you like.'

'Not ours,' Compo smiled innocently. 'Family o' Gippos movin' in next door.'

For one satisfying instant she went quite white.

They left Sam on the doorstep untying his laces.

'Don't forget!' he called.

They took the van back to Sid at the caff. He walked round it three times.

Perhaps for luck.

Anyway it seemed to make him feel better.

He came with his apron white on his stocky body and embraced Clegg briefly.

'Get off, you daft sod,' Clegg said, deeply moved by the gesture.

It grew dark early that Thursday.

Sky like the skin of a plum before the pubs had closed.

Twice, as they wheeled Clegg's bike towards Sybil's, they heard thunder, distantly, behind the postcard factory.

'Me mam used to say that was God,' Foggy said, 'shifting furniture.'

'God,' Compo stated flatly, 'would have a labourer for heavy stuff like that.'

'O yes?' Foggy snorted. 'And then before He knew where He was it'd be negotiations with the Standing Joint Committee. Naturally his paternal attitude would get up their bolshevik little nostrils and that would be it. Bingo. They'd be picketing the gates of heaven and He'd be locked out of His own premises.'

'Good luck to 'em,' Compo said. 'I don't believe in Him anyway.'

'And in His place,' Foggy continued, 'the silly sods would have no more sense than to elect the devil, on account of his overalls and his sly way with a few socialist clichés.'

Sybil's bedroom light was still on.

Could she be reading?

Some advanced manual of applied bitchery?

They wheeled the bike past the bungalow and stood uncertainly on the street corner.

It was gone eleven.

Past cocoa time in local suburbia.

Some of the bungalows still had their living room lights on. Displaying their innards shamelessly through picture windows. Carefully neat interiors in bright colours. Like bijou furnishing store windows.

'We ought to be in bed,' Foggy announced, 'not lurking about here.'

'Not all that excitin' being in bed,' Compo said. 'Not by theesen. Dun't exactly send thee ring all a twitter.'

'It's not madly exhilarating round here,' Foggy pointed out. 'And what are we going to say if a constable walks past?'

'How about – good evening, constable?' Clegg suggested.

Sybil's light went out. They decided to wait another fifteen minutes.

They passed very slowly as if the hour was constipated. Cars revved occasionally through the main street below them. More lights went out. The thunder sounded no nearer.

Last season's husband came out of a gateway with a dog. They watched his face in the street lights he passed but he gave them scarcely a glance. His dog had more curiosity and peed on Clegg's rear wheel.

'It likes you,' Compo said.

'Couldn't it just wag its bloody tail?'

They advanced on Sybil's wrought-iron outer defences. Anybody seeing them would just have thought – three old men behaving suspiciously.

Foggy paused with his hand on the gate and whispered. 'Can anybody remember if this thing creaks?'

Compo gave it a shove.

It did.

'It does,' he said.

Foggy dug him savagely in the brisket. 'Why are you such a ferkin' idiot?'

'Practice,' Compo said.

After a minute they emerged from the shadow of the hedge. They opened the gate by inches and wheeled Clegg's bike down the path, past the side door and round the back to Sam's bedroom window.

The demon lover was waiting. With his cap on and a coat over his flannelette pyjamas. Broad, deckchair stripes.

Clegg flashed his torch. 'I've got to tell you, Sam. You don't look as if you've got all that animal magnetism.'

'What are taking me in?'

'In nothing,' Clegg said, pointing to his bike. 'On.'

Sam's face fell. He pulled a pair of trousers over his pyjamas and put his slippers back on. The effort left him gasping for breath. In the stillness it sounded terrifyingly loud.

'Can't you postpone the heavy breathing?' Clegg suggested nervously.

'I have to breathe,' Sam protested indignantly.

'It's just a habit.' Clegg pulled a rug over the window-sill to preserve Sybil's paint. 'You could break it if you tried.' Clegg climbed halfway in and stuck despite a push from behind.

A behind and a half Compo was thinking as he leaned his weight against it. He probed with a bony index finger for the right critical area, found it and poked.

Clegg leapt two feet higher and cracked his head on the window top. He held his head through his cap and leaned out of the window to curse Compo with clenched teeth. 'You great dozy twat.'

'It got thee inside din't it?'

'It bloody did get me inside and that's the last suppository I ever want with a fingernail on it.'

'I can hear you round this side of the house,' Foggy whispered nervously, coming back from a roving sentry tour. 'What are you doing?'

'He's got a hundred and one ways of making your eyes water, that sod,' Clegg told him, adjusting the trim of his crotch.

They began to feed Sam through the window. After a false start, Clegg got him to sit on the sill with his feet inside the room and then pushed him backwards.

He went beautifully.

They wheeled him out of the gate and broke into a trot.

It was nearly two hilly miles to Sugden Street with a detour to avoid the main road and its too bright lights and police station. 'What am I doing here?' Sam was enquiring, 'an old man in poor condition with the wind whistling through the imperfectly adjusted flies of me pyjamas.'

57

'Shut up!' they told him, 'and just steer.'

But Clegg was thinking – as he glanced at unparalleled pale Sam – with slippered feet dangling – his cap at an impotent angle – if there is a Lord, have mercy on this damn fool ailing man being wheeled on a bicycle to an unwise assignation with no socks on.

It began to piss it down.

So all right be like that.

They passed:

The drummer from The Purple Lint Machine on his way home from a practice gig at the St John Ambulance hut where he'd had a pig of a night having twice to stand in for a Collis fracture thereby missing his turn for the mike not to mention the groupie who had to be in bed by half past nine. Dressed in the best clothes of an Afghan tribesman he walked against the rain with his shoulders stooped and fantasized of places with enormous cool and massive amplification where the last thing you'd ever see would be three old farts pushing a fourth on a beat-up bike. All I want – he hinted to a god of vague Asiatic appearance – is a place where they'd dig me with eye shadow and maybe a few spangles round me navel.

The house where West Riding Studio's Mr Crabtee was taking certain bedroom studies of his wife, an embarrassed lady who refused to come out from under the pillow.

Micklethwaite's with a light on in the kitchen where Micklethwaite had dropped off in his chair and his stocking feet and was snoring. An event which his wife, as always, was celebrating as a minor holiday.

*   *   *

Old Lady Froggatt after her fourteenth Guinness with the rain streaming down from her hat as she stepped hurriedly back from the road she was crossing to get out of their path as they shot past at a brisk canter with Sam ringing the bell and Foggy not pausing but raising his hat.

And they ran into Mervyn Stonehouse as he whipped round the corner in the invalid car that he borrowed sometimes from lame Uncle Desmond who – if not of a generous disposition – was very slow on his feet when it came to a race for the ignition key. Despite last minute slithering and braking they clouted the offside door with a scraping bang and Sam found himself spreadeagled on the vehicle roof, ignoring the weird surging of the blood in his veins, but worrying only about the dull ache in his balls; thinking sadly of the implications of unroad-worthiness in this department when so close to his goal.

'You bloody hooligans,' said Mervyn Stonehouse, staring at the dents in Uncle Desmond's door and looking bleakly into his own future where he could see some nasty wooden footwork. 'Get this old bugger off me roof.'

'He's not well,' Clegg said. 'We'll get him off in our own time.'

The windscreen wiper was still operating. Each time its blade passed within millimetres of Sam's nose. He adjusted to its rhythm and raised his face tiredly as it slid underneath. 'Will you either turn this thing off else tie a bloody hanky to it?'

They lifted him clear, set his cap straight and lowered him once again into the saddle. He winced at the contact of the hard, wet seat.

Compo opened the driver's door. 'Listen, fartface. There's enough death on the road without mad bleedin' cripples tearin' round corners as if they've got another leg they want to lose.'

'He's buckled your front wheel,' Foggy reported.

'I daren't think what he's done to my front fork,' said Sam, feeling the affected region gingerly.

Stonehouse closed his door and decided to conceal his wholeness if only for insurance purposes.

Clegg and Foggy finished checking Sam for signs of injury which wasn't easy while propping him up on the bike.

'Maybe it's just me,' Foggy sighed. 'But I'm growing increasingly disenchanted with this whole unseemly expedition.'

'I'm all right,' Sam said, looking far from it. 'Just get me there.'

'You've got some very frivolous motivations,' Foggy accused, 'for an invalid. On top of which your fly's undone.'

'I thought it were draughty coming downhill.'

They adjusted Clegg's cycling cape around him to keep him dry as well as they could. It was a bright glossy yellow.

'You look like a daffodil,' Clegg told him. He could see that Sam's slippers were wet and his feet felt like frozen food. He shook his head in disbelief and stared into Sam's determined white face. 'Are you sure it's worth it?'

'Just get me there, Norman,' Sam said.

Clegg turned his attention to Stonehouse who was busy swapping insults with Compo. They were exchanging everything but names and addresses.

'It's Mervyn Stonehouse,' Clegg announced. 'Driving his Uncle Desmond's three-legged noddy wagon. Badly. How long have you been driving like a fart, Mervyn? Is it a gift or have you been studying it?' He satisfied himself that the youth was unhurt, and they parted on those sort of terms. Each too embarrassed to want to involve the police.

They pushed Sam, lumpily now with a kink in his front wheel, into the darkness and the rain and Mervyn Stonehouse, pseudo-cripple, wafted after them a series of energetic, heartfelt V signs.

'Bloody cripples,' Compo snorted. 'Crutches aren't fast enough for 'em. Have to go bombin' round on three wheels.'

Compo looked down past the nine of spades to where his left leg ended in a froth of lace. Foggy, with a triumphant flourish despite the trouble he was having with his shoulder straps, played the jack.

Clegg trumped it.

'Well bugger me,' said Foggy. 'But what can you expect from a man wearing knickers the colour of that?'

Three pairs of underpants were steaming quietly by Lily's cheerful kitchen fire. Their outer garments were drying on a clotheshorse.

Dressed in an exotic lucky dip from Lily's airing cupboard, they were playing whist and drinking beer and wading through cheese and pickles.

'We'll get him a taxi back,' Clegg said.

They lifted their eyes heavenwards towards the bedroom floor and toasted Sam in his endeavours.

'I hope he's all right.'

'Can't be bad where he is.'

'You never know. You think you're doing nicely with what you've got in your hand then some bugger trumps it.'

'Don't get bitter and twisted.'

'I hope he hasn't gone through all that for a sexual disaster.'

'I believe,' Clegg said, 'in the capacity of Lily, Bless Her, to resurrect the flesh. Even after it's been battered a bit against an invalid carriage.'

'He only trapped it a bit. Not as if it were run over. If it had been run over we'd taken him home, wouldn't we?'

'Only place to be if your prong's been mauled on the highway. Whose deal?'

'Main thing is the tetsicles,' Compo announced. 'Long as they're alright tha's laughin'.'

'Tetsicles?'

'The nuts.'

'Tetsicles and nuts. Must be a new ice cream.'

'It's bollocks,' Compo said, reverting to the vernacular.

'Flavour of the month. Whatever next? That should improve a jaded sex life. Have you shuffled these?'

'The word is testicles – you little prawn.'

'That's what I said.'

'I beg to differ. Because when you said "tetsicles" you formed the mouth thus – and scattered bits of pickle and red cheddar in that general direction. Now had you said "testicles" you would have formed the mouth thus – and scattered bits of cheddar and pickle in this general direction.'

'Get stuffed,' said Compo with his mouth full.

The scream of Lily, Bless Her, ripped through their flimsy clothing, laid ice to their flesh and set its echoes churning through their innards. The next shriek freed them from their frozen immobility and they fell over the clotheshorse in their rush for the stairs door.

They found Lily, Bless Her, sobbing on the landing, wearing a see-through nightie over a practical warm vest.

Somehow indicative of the woman, Clegg thought. Frivolity tempered by something sounder.

She flung herself at them, her hair loose, her shoulders heaving. They appropriated the portions which Chance had allotted to them and patted them for comfort. And comfort them it did.

'He won't wake up,' she sobbed. 'It's Sam. He's dead.'

They tiptoed awestruck into the love nest.

The deceased lay smugly on a pastel mauve pillow, wearing a huge grin of contentment above his scraggy neck.

In the highest tradition of the hour of bereavement, they made a pot of tea.

They sat in the kitchen and sipped the scalding fluid. In silence. Gradually one fact of the immediate situation began to penetrate their confused deliberations.

Compo was slurping his tea.

'Shuttup,' said Foggy. 'You're not emptying a bloody bath.'

'I still can't believe it,' said Lily, Bless Her. 'I wouldn't have let him have me if I'd thought it was going to excite him like that.'

She raised the hem of her garment to wipe away a tear.

Their cups wobbled dangerously at the sight of the wealth of detail suddenly revealed.

Foggy hurriedly loaned her his handkerchief.

'I saw him lying there,' Clegg said. 'That familiar face, and I thought – Sam – you tactless prat!' He began to pace the frayed carpet, thoughtfully. 'Little sod! You can't trust anybody. We sneak him out. Once. And straightaway he goes off on this impulsive trip to the Infinite.'

'It'll be a shock for Sybil.'

'It'll be a shock for everybody if he's found here.'

'Fooling about being dead when he should be here, getting ready to go back to his own bed.'

'We were going to get him a taxi.'

'He ought to go back to Sybil,' Lily, Bless Her, said with a new note of determination in her voice. 'It's not right. I've never had much time for that woman but I wouldn't do this to her. He goes back. That's flat.'

'How?'

'Same way as you brought him. That's your lookout. I've never turned him away before, and I don't like doing it now, but I know where his place is at this moment and it's not here.'

She hadn't moved, but she'd changed, and they knew she meant it.

They went out in the yard to see if it was still raining. The air was clammy but it was technically fine.

'A taxi's no good now,' Foggy insisted.

Her Across snapped her outside light on and its beam trapped them like flies in amber.

They were still in their exotic Lilywear.

They scrambled frantically back in the house, leaving Her Across and her husband staring goggle eyed through wavering curtains and him thinking – God some of these creatures of pleasure are getting a bit rough. You're better off at home you are honest. In a surge of domestic harmony he reached up and gave Her Across a comradely feel.

64

She hit him with the kitchen clock.

'Be careful with him,' said Lily, Bless Her, and fled.

They peeled the bedclothes back from Sam, then hurriedly began looking for his pyjama bottoms.

'He wasn't all that badly injured then,' Compo said as they got Sam dressed. 'Poor bugger. He's only just got warm.'

They carried him downstairs. Even with the head dangling the grin remained constant.

Lily hid in the front room.

They took Sam into the kitchen.

So far he had been reasonably tractable.

They brought the bike in to practise a few positions.

They tried supporting him in the saddle but it was like trying to get hold of butter in a hot pan. They sat him on the handlebars and laid him back against the rider in the saddle. It would work going uphill, but then who could pedal? And going downhill would pitch him straight over the front wheel.

'We've got to get him home in reasonable condition,' Foggy said, and leaped to field Sam who was sliding down the fridge where they'd propped him while they discussed tactics. 'He's going to be in a hell of a state if he keeps falling off all the way home.'

'Drape him over the saddle,' Compo suggested. 'Like they do in the Westerns. Cowboys allus carry dead 'uns slung over a norse.'

A bit overcome by this rash of helpfulness from such a source, they tried it and stepped back to consider a Sam with his nose and his legs dangling on their respective sides of Clegg's rear wheel.

It looked a bit conclusive.

Nobody seeing him was going to believe they were just transporting home a drunk.

'Besides – look where his nose is.'

'Aye. Be awkward if he got it in the spokes.'

'Not only that – it's just exactly where that blasted dog peed.'

They couldn't do it to him.

'And anyway – if he stiffens like that they'll have to cram him in a V-shaped coffin.'

Thus it was that, moments later, Clegg pedalled wonkily on a buckled front wheel away from Lily, Bless Her's, in quest of Sid and another loan of the mauve and mobile chip emporium.

His tyres crackled wetly on the road. Though he was sweating, the town was cool after the rain. He could smell the enfolding hills.

Lord – he challenged – as he sped down Finkle Street – past a poster by sodium light of a girl in a bikini in the travel agent's window – past Smallpage's Aprons and Industrial Socks – past the bare white-tiled interior of Acaster's Family Butchers – remember what I asked on behalf of Sam? It must be admitted that at time of going to press you've made a right balls of everything – but now's your chance. Receive Sam Mordroyd kindly. With as much charity as he – if he were All Powerful and Omnipotent and had you before him lost and insignificant, a small ex-joiner and adulterer – would offer in his instinctive generosity to you.

St Hilda's clock unwound a quarter. With squeaks developing in the quaver of his front wheel he went throught the lights at yellow.

Not all the town was yet asleep.

66

West Riding Studio's Mr Crabtree was purring seductively to his wife through a pillow. At Mosely's Funeral Directors and Hire Cars the night taxi man was eating his sandwiches in the Chapel of Rest. Young Byron Pilbeam was reading feverishly. The drummer from The Purple Lint Machine was squeezing his blackheads in the bathroom. Micklethwaite was prodding his wife in her ample bosom while interrogating her about the appearance of an Irish penny in the day's takings and she, from force of habit, was taking it silently but thinking – according to telly at least in a police interrogation they do it in pairs and you get one who isn't a loud-mouthed bugger. Mrs Beever's Eva was lying in bed and reconstructing, while rubbing her knee, the conversation she'd overheard earlier between a Mrs Rettishaw and Mrs Edna Hepple concerning the lack of rigidity of Mr Hepple's prong. I wouldn't mind said Mrs Hepple discontentedly if only he'd leave it alone altogether but he will keep trying and then plays hell when it flops about like an anglepoise lamp. And Eichmann, over a beer in a caravan, was explaining to a colleague how the bottom was falling out of the hand-blended shit market.

Ivy dug a plump but powerful elbow in the kidneys of the just about sleeping Sid.

When the pain had subsided he turned wearily and in the light from the street, he found her sitting up in bed with shoulders like a wrestler under her curlers – her head cocked – her ears waiting to be loaded.

She hissed an Ivy whisper that made the stuff on the dressing table shiver. 'Listen! There's somebody at the window.'

'Don't talk wet. We're on the second floor.'

But his confidence suffered a setback when they saw a hand appear in silhouette and begin tapping on the glass.

'O my God!' said Ivy, and clutched the poor substitute of Sid. 'Go and see what it is.'

'And be a male, chauvinist pig?' Sid clutched her firmly back. 'What about all this equal opportunity?'

She shoved him out of bed and repulsed his attempts to clamber back.

'You bloody worm. Expecting your wife to go. Into the clutches of some escaped lunatic. Desperate for a woman.'

'Well there you are you see. It's for you.'

He made another attempt to get back into the warmth and safety.

He picked himself off the floor. 'Look at this rationally,' he said, straightening his pyjama flies which had become twisted round his hip. 'You're bigger than I am. And twice as nasty.'

The hand perked open, grabbed and swayed. They saw the fingers clawing desperately at the glass, then sliding down the full length of the pane with a despairing squeak. It disappeared and they heard a crash.

'O God! Mebbe there's more than one.' She patted her curlers. Head full of screaming headlines. THING RAVISHES YORKSHIRE HOUSEWIFE.

I shall never dare show meself at another Tupperware party. If I'm clutching me mother's photo mebbe they'll spare me.

'All we've seen so far is a hand,' Sid said encouragingly. 'The Phantom Finger. Worst that can happen up to now is that you'll be groped to death.'

He ducked the flying pillow and crept cautiously to the window.

'I'll remember you – you rotten sod. Expecting me to show meself half naked at the window. Inflaming him whatever it is.'

'Half naked? In that? There's enough stuff in one a your nighties to damp his flame down. He could wander about in there for a month and never find his way to a waterhole.'

He could just make out the shape of Clegg in a flower bed, disentangling his feet from a bicycle.

'You can relax,' he picked the pillow up and threw it back. 'It's nobody with an ungovernable urge to bite your bottom.' He goosed her as he went past the bed. 'Apparently the word's not got round yet what a fabulous arse you've got.'

He turned at the door. 'It's Clegg.'

'What does he want?'

'I'm going to find out, aren't I?'

* * *

For Clegg, the shape of Ivy at the window in a heavy-duty nightie as if a cloud had obscured a moon.

Sid unbolted the front door and showed his bare feet and his naked curiosity.

'I thought mebbe I could just wake you without disturbing Ivy.'

'Well I've got news for you. You made a right cock up of that.'

'Me bike slipped.'

'Before then. She's got ears like a bat. If I could train her to bark I'd be into a fortune.'

Clegg beckoned Sid into the garden with a glance upstairs which said not for Ivy's consumption.

Despite the unpleasant wet sensations on his feet, Sid followed thinking – Jesus what cronies I do have.

Ivy saw them whispering together. Saw the upturned, guilty, up-to-no-good face of her husband checking instinctively on her whereabouts.

She put on her dressing-gown from the back of the door, shoved her plump feet into sensible slippers and went downstairs.

But Clegg had gone.

Sid sat through his Ivy grilling still half in shock. What could you tell her? She'd never understand that you can't refuse a late mate the use of your chip van. Clegg knew. Crafty dog. But if he gets caught, the sod, and word gets round about what's being transported in me van. Christ Almighty won't me sales plummet? I mean folk are just naturally going to think twice before they start splashing vinegar with any abandon on anything that comes out of that stable.

'Are you even listening to me?'

He looked into the hard blue eyes in the soft, still sometimes pretty face.

'Am I talking to me sen? What did he come here for at this time?'

'He came to tell me Sam's dead. Sam Mordroyd.'

'Are you sure that's all?'

'It's enough to be going on with in't it – being dead?'

'You know what I mean. It's a funny time to tell anybody. It's not as if you're related. There's summat else. It's bloody funny him coming here this time a night then skittling off before I can get to him.'

'Rubbish. You've had that effect on every bloke I know.'

'You know such bloody rogues,' she said, putting the kettle on. 'I can't say I'm surprised about Sam. Mrs Lutterworth said he were very poorly. It'll be a shock for his wife though.'

'Not as much as it might have been,' Sid said.

She watched him suspiciously as he stared unblinkingly at the fridge door.

They took the tea to bed.

O God, Sid prayed. Don't let 'em mangle me van. He sipped his tea noisily.

'Manners!' Ivy corrected.

And if SHE finds out, I'm dead.

'There should be no secrets,' Ivy said sulkily, 'between a husband and wife.'

'That's rich coming from you. Some bugger who always get undressed behind the wardrobe door. Hoppin' about on one bloody leg sooner than let me have a lamp at your infinite variety.'

'Subject normal,' Ivy adjusted her nightdress with the air of a miser locking his safe. 'Just like me mother said. You'll want to look at wallpaper and all they're interested in is the rolls of fat at the top of your leg.'

'On behalf of all we bum-and-tit men,' Sid protested, 'allow me to point out that your mother's unreliable in sexual matters. I mean look at your dad.'

'And while we're on about modesty,' Ivy picked off his exploring hand as if it were a glove and let it drop, 'I should appreciate a bit more from you. It gives me no girlish pleasure I might tell you to see you always dangling prominently around the bedroom. If you think it stokes the fires of me lust you can forget it. With a forty-eight waist, you're nobody's idea of thunder in the blood.'

She turned her back towards him.

He ran his hand about it.

Me favourite view.

She may not be easy but by God she's wide.

It's all good stuff if only she'd relax a bit.

What every man needs: his own few familiar acres.

He kissed her between the shoulder and the neck and lacerated his face on her curlers.

He gave it up and settled down for sleep.

A cat howled weirdly among the back gardens.

I wish him better luck than I'm having.

I must be mad, he decided, letting Clegg talk me into that. Poor old Sam. You think about life after death but you never think it's going to mean falling into the hands of them three dozy buggers.

The smuggled Sam out of Sugden Street in Lily's bedroom carpet which left him fluffy but unseen. Lily,

Bless Her, followed with his cap.

They had to unwrap him when they got him in the van to thread him round the centre pillar of the big cupboard.

Lily lowered her eyes and shivered in her dressing gown.

It's like he's being buried already, she concluded.

Me last look at Sam.

She peeped and saw him in stark torchlight being rolled in among the potatoes.

And he still hasn't put me that plug on.

It's true what Maureen said. All them years ago.

If you're going to win at this game, Lily, you'll have to start getting the money first.

I've always been sloppy at the economic side.

Must check if Warburton's just as useless with other implements.

She saw them close the cupboard doors and straighten up to catch their breath.

She broke down a little when Foggy fastened his little flag to the wobbly aerial, slid it to half mast and removed his hat.

She gave them a grateful hug.

Which could have been why Clegg grated the cogs three times before he found first gear; and which was certainly why the other two didn't even notice.

They left her waving sadly on the pavement: a finger of breeze probing indelicately through her clothing.

They rode the mauve emporium.

Subjective sad music in their heads but mainly the fear of their own daring in transporting illegally the no longer quite Sam.

They saw the constabulary in every shadow.

Clegg chose another devious route and fought the van's desire to mount the pavement.

Foggy discovered that the pans were not quite cold.

'He's not going to get too warm under there, is he?'

'He's not going to be there long enough, is he?'

'Tha knows what to do if he gets too hot,' Compo giggled nervously. 'Just roll him in batter.'

'I find that very distasteful,' Foggy reproved.

'O give over. Sam could tek a joke.'

'He could dish one out an all,' Clegg said. 'Look at the bloody mess he's dropped us in.'

'We'll have him home in a minute,' Compo encouraged. 'If Fitipaldi here gets his finger out and stops scrapin' that gear stick about. Tha's supposed to drive it not row the bloody thing.'

'Keep him quiet back there,' Clegg ordered Foggy. 'If you will ride about with a retarded dwarf least you can do is keep him under control.'

'I thought he was with you.'

'I've had no use for him since I got rid of the barrel organ.'

'Bollocks to you lot,' Compo said. 'I'll talk to Sam.'

They passed Ossie Basset's lorry, parked outside his house; loaded and ready for an early start. Clegg steered ponderously round, throwing them off balance.

'Hey up!' Compo protested. 'Why don't you make a noise through your lips? You're drivin' like a fart.'

'I want to get him home,' Clegg said. 'He's not all that portable but at least he's pliable. Let's get him there before he packs even that in.'

'It's hard to believe,' Foggy pointed out, 'that only a couple of hours ago he was as well as could be expected

74

on the roof of an invalid carriage.'

'Look,' Clegg said. 'He went the way he wanted to go.'

'He went the way every bloke wants to go,' Compo said with feeling.

They pondered the implications of being accessories to Sam's novel suicide.

As they bounced past the road works in Allison Street, the top third of Sam came out of the cupboard and flopped across Compo's welly.

Compo panicked and scrambled on to the serving counter, recalling THE HAND OF THE MUMMY and CURSE OF THE VAMPIRE vividly.

'Listen,' Clegg said. 'Don't start getting stand-offish with Sam. You've never backed off him before. Don't start getting prejudiced 'cos he's dead.'

'He grabbed me welly,' Compo shuddered. 'We'll see how tha likes a dead man's hand then, clever bugger.'

He trailed two of his own fingers down the back of Clegg's neck.

Clegg yelped and screwed the van into a violent swerve. Compo cackled merrily.

Foggy clapped a hand over Compo's mouth, thinking even in his nervousness, I shouldn't be touching it. God knows where it's been. I'd rather handle Sam.

'Will you pack it in for Christ's sake?' He wiped his hand on Compo's jacket. 'We could have had an accident.'

'We nearly did,' Compo pointed at Clegg. 'He nearly shit his sen.'

They rolled Sam back into the cupboard. Foggy anticipating a policeman's hand on his collar every minute. Thinking—

The scandal of it.

Us three in Madame Tussaud's next to Burke and Hare.

Serves me right for lowering me social tone.

But what a prospect for eternity. Me a wax figure alongside this dozy prick.

He elbowed Compo into a corner.

'Now behave yourself.'

He looked at his watch. Quarter past two. His landlady would be frosty at the breakfast table.

There would be a hard moral edge to the fried bread.

Clegg experimented with a few switches looking for the dip in case he needed main beam. Apologizing mentally to Sam.

No offence, mate.

Just that there's been an indefinable change in our relationship.

It's you that started it.

If you're going to be dead all the time you're going to have to get used to this sort of thing.

He switched the wipers off for the third time.

Did you have to go rushing into it?

Is there something going off over there we ought to know about?

Are the hills of eternity green? Is there unpolluted crystal water?

It won't be for me if there aren't any trees.

Does he regret it already?

No more rambles up Leatherby way or leisurely through Lily, Bless Her.

It's a sod how irreversible everything is.

They rolled to a quiet stop three bungalows down from Sybil's.

Clegg switched off the engine and sat a moment, listening.

Just the breeze rustling the bushes and the steady drone of Compo and Foggy being offensive to each other in subdued but fervent undertones.

For Christ's sake, Sybil, have a topping night's sleep.

All sounds this night are essentially friendly.

It's only us bringing your husband home.

He came out of the cupboard easier than he went in.

The rolled him in the rug and coughed quietly at the ascending fluff.

The street was still empty.

They tucked the woolly Sam under their arms and set off awkwardly from the van.

'Get in step,' Foggy hissed.

'I wouldn't mind,' Compo whispered, 'if he'd been int Guards or summat. But when were they ever in step int Royal Bloody Signals?'

The gate was open as they'd left it.

They held their breath and tiptoed down the path, treading on each other's feet but resisting the instinct to moan about it.

They were enormously aware of Sybil's bedroom window. As if she were coiled in there, like a cat, waiting to spring.

They froze, petrified as the lights of a car bisected the darkness of the street.

They dropped Sam hurriedly and followed him down; their noses inches from the path.

'That's all we need,' Foggy whispered. 'A police panda car. Cries of, "Hello, hello, what time of night is this for three ageing carpet salesmen".'

The lights steadied as the vehicle stopped. They heard

the engine stop. The lights flicked off.

They swallowed.

'Listen, we just happened to be passing in Sid's chip van,' Clegg hissed urgently, 'when we had this premonition. In fact it was a voice. An unearthly voice. Said – Go at once to Hillcrest View and make enquiries regarding Sam. We obeyed. And when we got there we found him stretched out here.'

'Obviously expecting us.'

'Don't piss about,' Clegg said. 'If you can think up owt better now's your chance.'

'What about the rug?' Compo reminded him. 'Did the voice tell us to wrap him in a bastard rug?'

'And if it did,' Foggy added scornfully. 'Did it tell us where we could find one at short notice covered in all this bloody fluff?'

He fought the urge to sneeze.

They heard a car door: voices and footsteps.

They felt an overpowering urge to get up and begin running.

Me suit, Foggy realized, is going to be in ratty condition. If we get hauled off to the nick they're never going to accept me plea of superior social position.

He could feel the damp seeping through from the path.

O God let me collar still be clean.

They heard a garage door being opened. Then the sounds of the car being put away.

'It's only somebody been out late,' Compo got to his feet.

They grabbed Sam and tiptoed round the back.

'They must have seen the chip van,' Foggy said.

'That's not a felony,' Clegg made sure he climbed all

the way into the bedroom this time, staying well clear of Compo's lifting finger.

He pulled Foggy in after him.

They stood for a moment listening. The house was quieter than the world outside.

It smelled of furniture polish.

Compo unwrapped Sam and they hauled him inside and on to the bed.

They drew the curtains, checked that the bedroom door was closed and switched on a light.

It had to be admitted that Sam looked terrible.

You sod – Clegg thought. You haven't been dead five minutes and look at you.

His face and his pyjama jacket were stained from his brush with the potatoes. His trousers were covered in fluff.

They grabbed a handful each and gave a tug.

The tractable Sam bumped noisily on to the floor.

They stood absolutely still in horror, their shoulders hunched as if expecting a blow. They heard movement in Sybil's bedroom.

Clegg switched off the light.

'What are you doing thumping about?'

'Answer her,' Foggy whispered.

'You answer her.'

'Have you dropped something?' There was a new note of concern in her voice.

'Get off to sleep,' Clegg mumbled quickly through his hand.

'I can't hear you,' she said.

The pause seemed never ending before she spoke again.

'Are you all right?'

'Yes,' Clegg shouted nastily in what to him was a miserable imitation of Sam's voice.

'Don't lose your rag,' Sybil rose to the challenge. 'I only asked. We're going to have to come to some agreement me and you if I'm going to be nursing you. We're going to have to have an understanding. You're going to have to stop fighting me every hand's turn. Do you hear? Are you listening?'

Clegg made the noise of a loud yawn.

'You better get your sleep,' she said. 'I'm not having you lolling about in bed all day. You've been going to do that sink unit for eighteen months. Well now you've got that time you always reckoned you were short of.'

After a tense two minutes of silence they began to lift Sam back on the bed.

Foggy switched the light on again.

They exchanged a nervous glance.

Compo poked his head through the curtains. 'Sod me.' He looked at Clegg pointedly. 'Not only drives like a clown but does imitations.'

They pulled Sam's trousers off and handed them to Compo with instructions to take himself off somewhere quietly and shake them.

Foggy was depressed by his own appearance in the wardrobe mirror.

All the gloss gone.

Night like this he realized knocks three kinds of shit out of your military bearing.

Clegg was working on Sam with the edge of a blanket; wiping his face and flicking the potato earth stains from his pyjamas. He pointed to the brush and comb on the dressing table and Foggy began tidying Sam's hair.

Through it all Sam continued to grin as if he found it enormously amusing.

In the street, Compo was waving a pair of trousers defiantly at the world. He thumped them for good measure several times against a lamp post. Suddenly, as an afterthought, he went through the pockets.

A handkerchief.

A folded piece of fine sandpaper.

Three pound notes.

And a packet of Park Drives.

Compo helped himself to a cigarette which he tucked behind his ear. It was much the worse for wear.

I'm a right twat I am – he decided – in a fit of self-criticism – not checkin' afore I bounced 'em on that lamp.

He put everything else back in Sam's pockets and tiptoed again down Sybil's path.

They left Sam comfortable in his bed.

After they returned the van to the waste ground, before they parted to go their respective ways, they paused a moment; remembering Sam's face as they'd left it on his pillow.

'He never looked so good.'

'Except he's dead,' Foggy pointed out.

'But only just,' Clegg said.

In the sky above the city, the sullen cumulus reflected light in the colours of the belly of a fish.

Friday morning after a cool start the wind veered into the south. Blue broke through the overcast in places. Weather forecasts spoke of bright periods.

That's a laugh – thought the bird at the cleaners who had given up expecting hers, and was tuning the dial in search of moody music.

The Gas Board began diggings in Allison Street.

A man called Baddeley bit the hand of a traffic warden outside the Post Office.

In the basement of Calvin Oates & Son, Solicitors and Commissioners for Oaths, a junior clerk picked his way through cobwebby bundles and sang reflectively of his love for the big Kawasaki 900cc.

Sybil visited the Co-operative Funeral Services at 14 High Street (or any Grocery Branch).

Acaster slipped the point of a knife between two slices of roast pork and flipped the top one expertly on to his scales.

Mr Travis Slingsby MCHS was messing about with people's feet.

Mrs Beever's Eva tucked her skirt into her navy blue knickers and did cartwheels at the request of the Pearson brothers.

Foggy went shopping for his landlady.

Micklethwaite got rid of his Irish penny to the breadman.

Sid carried out a very careful inspection of his chip van.

The drummer from The Purple Lint Machine rejected Christianity and resolved to embrace Zen and get up before dinner time.

Clegg took his washing to the launderette and sat in the window waiting, reading the Order of the Burial of the Dead.

West Riding Studio's Mr Crabtree awaited his third bride of the week at the churchyard, thinking, God preserve us from any more friends of the groom with a bastard Pentax.

Lily, Bless Her, struggling to fix the plug on her vac, discovered at her plump inner thigh a run in her tights and became temporarily depressed at the intractability of things.

Compo studied a list of runners at the betting shop.

Byron Pilbeam gazed in wonder through the windows of Freeman, Hardy and Willis at a salesman kneeling before the waving knees and bloomers, and handling the knotty but unmistakably feminine legs of a customer, and felt his O-level drives receding at the stirring of a true vocation.

They met in Sid's caff. Foggy with his landlady's groceries; Clegg his laundry: Compo with a page smuggled out from the betting shop.

They got three teas from Ivy, who tried to question Clegg in probing Ivy tones, but lost him somewhere in the evasiveness of his own, long marital experience.

They sat at a far table near the window.

Watched the Friday bustle in the street.

'I was dog tired,' Foggy said. 'But could I hell as sleep.'

'A can of ale,' Compo said without raising his eyes

83

from his paper. 'Last thing before tha goes to bed. Works a treat.'

'I kept thinking about Sam,' Foggy said.

'Snag is,' Compo interrupted again. 'Sometimes it gets thee up for a pee.'

Foggy ignored him. 'One disquieting thought in particular.'

Clegg looked at him as if he knew what was coming.

'Apart from the bog up me trousers were in,' Foggy went on. 'I refer,' he said, holding his teacup delicately in pointed contrast to Compo's clutching fist, 'to the strong possibility that if we'd left him alone yesterday, he might still be alive.'

'No doubt about it,' Clegg conceded. 'He wouldn't have snuffed it half so quickly in Sybil's care.'

Ivy was earwigging. Her ministrations with a damp cloth ever drawing nearer.

They sat her out in silence until she ran out of things to wipe and flounced huffily back to the counter.

'You admit it then!' Foggy said.

'Certainly. Of course he was going to live longer with Sybil. You know what the doctors told him. No excitement. Well that's as good as writing Sybil on the prescription.'

'True,' said Compo. 'Medicine as nasty as that's bound to do you some good.'

'And furthermore,' Clegg added, 'there's the psychological factor. The more you want to go the less you can rely on doing it. It's like the elusive erection in advancing middle age.'

'I hope this poxy hoss falls flat on his bastard face this time,' said Compo, tapping his paper.

After a scathing glance at the less than glossy follower

of the sport of kings, Foggy sought Clegg's eyes.

'And it doesn't worry you?'

'He wanted to go.'

'Maybe last night. On impulse. In theory. But I bet he feels a right prawn this morning.'

'He knew what he was up to,' Clegg said. 'More than any of us.' He sipped his tea and stared through the window.

Traffic was snarled behind an articulated lorry at the lights.

'He launched himself from Lily, Bless Her, like a high cliff. You saw the grin. He knew who he'd laid on at the bottom to pick up the pieces.'

'I think I fancy Dandy's Castle,' Compo announced, 'to romp home three lengths in front of the opposition and buy me a new suit for the funeral.'

'That's a pernicious mixture of improvidence and respect,' Foggy told him. 'What if you lose?'

'You've got to be brave about it.'

'And what are you going to look like then at the funeral?'

Compo thought about it.

'Tatty?' he said.

'You don't need a new suit for the funeral,' Clegg said. 'Sam left you his.'

'Me?'

'You.'

'He did?'

'Yes.'

'That blue un?'

'That blue un.'

'Hey up. Not bad. Why din't tha say summat last night? I could a tekken it wi' me.'

They sat him up straight in his chair and gave him the message.

'Who's a dosy little twat then?'

'I bet that's me,' Compo said.

'He's recognized the description.'

'We didn't see Sam last night.'

'We never went near him.'

'We'd like to hear you repeat that.'

'We never went near him,' Compo said obligingly.

'That's why you couldn't tek the suit.'

'Because we weren't there.'

'Got it,' Compo said. He stood up. 'So let's nip up there now and get it.'

He disappeared under the table as they buffeted him with a rain of slaps.

After a while he emerged cautiously.

'What's up now?' he enquired in injured tones.

'We can't go up there and fetch the suit he left you yet – because nobody's told us that he's dead.'

'As far as we're supposed to know he's still alive.'

Compo pulled his cap down to his chin and used the privacy to do his mental calculations.

They watched the muscles moving beneath the material covering his face as he considered this most recent information.

Finally he raised the cap slowly and his puzzled features reappeared.

They waited for the response.

'Let him keep his bastard suit,' he said. 'If it's going to be all that trouble.'

They walked together as far as the bridge.

'Best thing we can do,' Clegg said, 'is go home and get

a bite a dinner. Then the thing is to behave naturally.'

'No need to overdo it,' Foggy elbowed Compo to stop him picking his nose.

'We'll hang about somewhere where we'll meet people.'

'Three Legs,' Compo said, quick as a flash.

'Bloody hell,' Foggy said. 'How long did it take you to think a that?'

'Just kem to me.'

'It'll do,' Clegg said. 'We're bound to meet somebody who'll inform us about Sam being dead. Then we can nip up there and pay our respects.'

'And fetch me suit.'

'And fetch his suit and check whether Sybil's got any suspicions which we can perhaps alleviate by a Christian willingness to lie like fury.'

Foggy sat down to sardines.

Infallible register of his landlady's acid factor.

The shopping hadn't mollified her.

He looked down at the two small fish on his plate.

They weren't a meal so much as two ladylike fingers, deep in tomato sauce, being waved provocatively under his tash.

She poured him stewed, black tea.

Another doghouse indicator.

She watched him critically until he began to eat.

He remained conscious of her through the sound of toast crunching in his ears.

Lace blouse and wrinkles. Face powder like flour.

The dragon sister.

An oak-cased clock ticked wheezily on an oaken mantelpiece.

A room like chapel.

Potty spinster sister could be heard in the kitchen; singing.

Something about the trousers of the lord.

At least between tears she was sweeter.

Surely that must have been 'houses of the Lord'.

Dragon sister went away.

He pulled a face as the tea varnished his palate.

They were good digs. Spotless. Even refined.

The sauce bottle and the marmalade were always in their chrome containers and he appreciated that.

But sometimes . . .

The Yorkshire terrier waddled in to check on his menu. It looked like a small pig in a badly fitting wig.

'Absolutely not,' he told it, and quickly finished the single slice of toast. 'In fact if you don't watch it you candlewick prat, I shall be after you for your biscuits.'

Compo had chips and mushy peas, then wrote out his bet.

The bloke behind the grille flinched at the state of the bit of paper he was handed.

'What's this?' he asked, poking off some loose green stuff with the edge of his ruler. 'I didn't order these with all this vinegar on.'

'Don't piss about,' Compo said. 'Get it written down. Unless it's too big for thee.'

'Would you mind reading it out? As far as I can gather you want fish and chips twice on Dandy's Castle.'

'Tha's a laugh a minute, thee.' Compo produced his fag tin and lit up a tab. 'I wonder why it is the staff allus have so much rattle?'

'I'm sorry I can't get you the proprietor, but he's in Ibiza where he has to go three times a year just to unload some of the stuff that gets forced on him by you lot.'

'Some people give to Oxfam,' Compo shrugged. 'But I like to see where me money goes.'

'Dozy punters.' He put his glasses on and read the bet scornfully.

'How's he doing, the boss then?' Compo enquired.

'Very nicely thank you,' Glasses said.

'That's good,' Compo said, smiling with perfect charity.

'Except – that some Herbert keeps coming in and swiping pages from the office paper causing inconvenience to the other punters.' He raised his eyes from his ledger and stared over his glasses at Compo pointedly.

'What can tha expect?' Compo said. 'Tha gets such rubbish in here. Look at thee clientele.'

He accepted his betting slip through the grille and checked it.

'In fact ahm seriously thinkin' of tekkin all me business to somebody like William Hill.'

'If we can be of any assistance,' Glasses said, 'in affecting the change-over you've only got to ask.'

'A branch with a carpet,' Compo went on. 'And a proper picture on the wall. Not just that badly drawn cannon over yonder.'

They both knew he was referring to the obscene scrawl above the radiator.

'If we rubbed 'em all off,' Glasses said mournfully, 'we'd be through the bloody brickwork in a fortnight.'

'Tha must admit tha's due for decoration.'

'I deserve a medal. For consorting with you lot.'

'Redecoratin'.'

89

'We will if you will,' Glasses said, eyeing Compo's sartorial arrangements. Thinking didn't I see you in the graveyard scene in *David Copperfield*.

'You're on,' Compo challenged.

Or was it *Great Expectations*?

'Don't be surprised,' Compo sucked the last few millimetres of his fag end expertly, 'if the next time tha sees me, I'm all tarted up in me best navy blue. I don't allus,' he informed Glasses as he ground what was left of his tab under his welly, 'swan about in me working clobber.'

'Working clobber?' Glasses spluttered. 'When did you ever have a job?'

'Wi' Muriel,' Compo said at the door. 'She packed a right wallop did Mew. I had a job wi' her.'

Clegg rinsed his plate and his beaker.

Left them on the draining board.

He took his pipe into the tiny, paved garden.

He was on a level with the massive eye of the church clock fifty yards away.

Seven minutes to one o'clock.

Although according to the radio God was two minutes slow.

Nobody's perfect.

Sparrows were chirping over children's voices. He could hear the noise of the partial market which always preceded Saturday.

The sky was blue around the church tower. He saw the clock's gilt hand lurch thickly through another minute.

If there was a God – would he have time – he wondered – for a middle-aged man in baggy trousers over sensible boots digesting a sausage roll?

*   *   *

90

They went to the Three Legs.

Five halves of beer each later they left having learned:
that Lockerby's hourly rate for unskilled labour was going up by two and a half pence;

that the council had condemned Lower Gowthorpe Street;

that Austin Hinchcliffe had been named Co-Respondent of the Year by a panel of his workmates at E. G. Babcock Builders;

that Leeds had no chance next season;

that Eichmann had no faith in the future of solar energy but had heard rumours of some genius in Derby who was running his Land Rover on henshit;

that the tiniest fence of black lace at the bottom of the barmaid's cleavage seemed to be all that was preventing her livestock from wandering;

that Mrs Turnbull's lodger had every reason to be satisfied with his five pounds a week;

that Dandy's Castle was a camel;

how Vernon Briggs cured his dandruff

the dirty devil;

the rudiments of the Wally Batty formula for bringing a sheen to the feathers of a pigeon;

where Bramley Dugdale was when needed at the Fire Station;

where Mrs Woodstock was feeling the pain;

how the skin round Beefy Evans's navel seemed to stay where you poked it after his seventh pint;

but not a word concerning Sam or Sybil.

They discussed this while they were standing in the toilets.

After five halves, there's time.

During which their attention wandered.

'Funny system when you think about it,' Clegg said looking down. 'Having taps at your disposal. Queer really.'

'Mine's all right,' Compo protested.

'I'm speaking generally,' Clegg soothed him. 'Don't get gladiatorial about it. Although come to think about it, it was the weapon Sam chose. To end it all. Just as surely as if he'd stuck it in his ear and blown his brains out.'

Foggy winced a little at this imagery. 'Do you mind!'

'Christ!' said Compo picturing the event vividly.

Even Clegg was a shade startled by the spectre he'd raised. He began to look at things differently.

'Never saw it in a sinister light before,' he shuffled nervously. 'Always saw it as essentially comic. I mean look at it. Again I'm speaking generally, I hasten to add.' He gave Compo a shove back to his own stall. 'The common urge to snigger is sound. Surer than these artistic poses which pretend to wax lyrical about it.'

'Put it away,' Foggy said. 'We came to bury Caesar not to praise him.'

'I'm just striving to view it in a baleful role,' Clegg explained. 'I could see it in a bread roll. It'd just be a hamburger. No wonder they call 'em private parts. Absolutely nothing officer like. Bananas.'

'And you,' Compo said.

'Bananas,' Clegg continued undeterred, 'are more aesthetically clad. Though I don't suppose we'd be all that keen on peeling 'em every time.'

'You shouldn't have had that last beer,' Foggy informed him.

'It looks like an ill-adapted reptile,' Clegg abandoned it to the darkness. 'I'll tell you what though. It's a guarantee of human steadiness. You'll see. We shall return gradually to the lumpish roots of our being.'

They went outside, blinking a bit in the light.

'Be not impressed,' Clegg advised, 'by all this talk about the sexual revolution. It's going to take more than fancy shirts, long hair, even an ornamental jangler. Because the illusion of trendiness comes a right pratfall when finally all you've got to whip is that old butter-fingered fumbling creature.'

They had a walk to Sugden Street.

Her Across gave them a look which was practically a citizen's arrest as they knocked at Lily, Bless Her's door.

But Lily, Bless Her, hadn't heard anything either.

They began to repair her flex, under the supervision of Sergeant Foggy, Royal Signals (ret'd).

'I laddered me tights with that damn thing,' said Lily, Bless Her. 'Look.'

They looked.

And Foggy got his wires crossed.

They went back to school.

Not with any conscious purpose but because, after they left Lily, Bless Her's, their feet took them there.

It was empty for the holidays.

Modern extensions had altered the shape but the old, stone core remained from their day.

They left the last of the beer in the boys' playground toilets. Performing in silence this time, nostalgically.

Reading the walls.

Spelling hadn't improved any.

They came out and sat on the playground walls, recalling the feel of brick through schoolboy trousers.

* * *

'The main difference is, growing up,' Clegg said, 'you get fewer scabs on your knees.'

A dog was sleeping in the sunlight on the pavement. The sun was warm on their backs.

Across the street, a woman opened a stiff bedroom window and shook a duster.

A kid with a dummy plugged into his slimy, serious face pedalled squeakily on a tin tricycle.

Somewhere a door opened allowing the voice of a disc-jockey to escape hysterically before it was recaptured and hauled shrieking back inside again.

A dustbin lid shivered metallically.

Compo removed his jacket and sat on it. 'Me pants,' he explained, 'are gettin' a bit thin. Tha could get blisters on thee arse off this brick.'

'Thin?' Foggy sniffed. 'They've got malnutrition, mate, to say the least of it.'

'True,' Compo admitted readily. 'I'm just about ready for that suit.'

'You're going to keep it for best I hope.'

Compo thought about it. His head cocked. Lips pursed.

'I trust you're not planning to wear it every day till it looks like everything else you've got. Sam's had it years,' Foggy continued, 'and it still looks like new.'

'Argh,' Compo agreed, 'but think on he did all his heavy work in pyjamas. Listen,' he said, getting enthusiastic, 'why don't we just nip up to Sybil's now, and say how do Sybil, we thought we'd pop in and visit owd Sam seein' as how we was passin' and she'll scream or summat and say he's dead like? And we'll say O hell or summat like that. Would you believe it? And if there's owt we can do Sybil like tek that owd suit off thee hands tha's only got to ask.'

He ducked Foggy's punch.

''Cos we'd have no chance,' Clegg said, 'trying to simulate surprise in the teeth of Sybil's nearly perfect perjury detector.'

'You'll just have to wait,' Foggy said. 'You've been tatty all your life. You were tatty when you were here.' He waved an arm to include the school. 'What's all this unseemly rush all of a sudden? This religious conversion to tailoring.'

'We were all tatty when we were here,' Compo said.

'Speak for yourself.' Foggy's hackles began to rise. Compo sneered.

'The Foggies maintained certain standards even though the Depression.'

'Tha were a right sisspot.' Compo turned to Clegg. 'He used to play more wit lasses than he did wi' us.'

'Play?' Foggy snorted. 'The things you used to get up to weren't play. There was Capone in Chicago, and you: obscene midget round here. Who cornered the market in bootleg yo-yos? And there were things went off in them lavatories . . .' He paused searching for words to do justice to his emotions.

'Half-penny bangers mostly,' Compo sniggered wheezily.

'Who put that horrible thing down Aileen Sanderson's knickers?' Foggy challenged.

'That wan't me,' Compo said.

'I know it wasn't you. It was a frog. I could tell the difference even in those days. Your mouth was bigger. But you put it down. There was no mistaking you anywhere.' Foggy pointed out. 'Not in them damn great boots.'

'I had to wear Our Kevin's cast offs.'

'Cast offs? Nobody cast off them great slumours. They might have heaved them to one side a bit that's all. Perhaps had 'em shunted by a chap with a lorry. O, I remember 'em vividly. And well I ought. I had 'em planted on me person often enough. Me mam used to say to me – Cyril, I don't know why you keep getting this rash on your chest. Rash? It was a bloody footprint. His idea of a morning's exercise was a swift trot up my clavicle.'

'Aye we had some fun,' Compo said, twisting his features and staring round the playground; the sounds of children in his head. 'Does tha' remember Sam wi' that grass snake?' He looked at their old classroom window. 'And that mornin' that little yellowhammer flew straight intut glass. I picked it up. They've got lovely markings. An' it had a drop a blood on its beak. One drop. Identical same colour as ours. It spilled on me fingernail and dried just like me own did.'

'I remember,' Clegg sighed. 'You'd think there'd be an amnesty for bonny things on sunny days.'

He thought about the one or two brightly plumed kids who had left school flying cheerfully but didn't get far.

Ran smack into World War Two.

Don Naylor lying in Africa somewhere. Blood on his beak. Identical same colour as ours.

I don't suppose it was a large proportion of our class register that they transferred later to the war memorial. But you don't like to think of any busy, vivid things being wasted like that.

'Yes,' he said, standing up and massaging the feeling

back into his buttocks. 'I remember Sam and that grass snake. Incipient leanings towards the phallic even then.'

They went home by way of the market.

Clegg bought a bit of lettuce for his tea.

They decided to have an early night.

Warburton that evening discovered Lily, Bless Her, almost all in black.

'O yummy,' he said to himself, and his heart capered adolescently.

But she wasn't having any.

'Not tonight,' she said. 'I can't. I'm that upset.'

She sent him home to his wife.

Who said, 'You're early dear, for Friday.'

'Mind your own rotten business,' he said. 'Look at yourself. Call that a dress? Why do you think I work every hour God sends if it's not to keep things nice? It may not have occurred to you, but I have a position to upkeep. Where's them black stockings I bought you? Why don't you wear them sometimes? You've stopped caring for me, haven't you? Yes you have. Else you wouldn't be wearing great thick things like these. Why don't you surprise me sometimes?' he said, grabbing her more firmly.

'You want a surprise,' she said, moving her mouth away. 'Well how's this for a start?' She removed his hand. 'Me mother's coming round in about ten minutes. And don't slam the door like that.'

Saturday was overcast, windless, cool.

Foggy wore his raincoat on his way to Clegg's.

He carried a newspaper and left Dragon Sister viewing at her window; the Potty One doing the beds.

Shoppers were dressed in Saturday better clothes.

He found Clegg in an old pullover, removing his bicycle front wheel and pieces of skin from his knuckles.

'Four letter words,' Clegg informed him, 'were a gift to the world from the first bloke who ever laid a spanner to an unyielding nut. And speaking of unyielding nuts – let us turn our thoughts to Northern Ireland and the Flat Earth Society.'

He gave the bike a swift kick.

'Of course there are those who maintain that Northern Ireland is the Flat Earth Society.'

'It's in last night's paper,' Foggy said.

'Well there you are then,' Clegg said, leading the way indoors and running his knuckles under the tap.

'About Sam.' Foggy thrust the folded paper under Clegg's chin, and pointed to the item.

'I haven't got me glasses. You'll have to read it.'

'Mordroyd – Samuel H.'

'Samuel H.?'

'Beloved husband of Sybil.'

'Must be another one.'

'At his home. Following a long illness. Funeral Monday. So it looks like,' Foggy dropped the paper on

98

the table, 'that we've had more luck than we deserve, and got away with it.'

'Samuel H.,' Clegg said, putting the kettle on.

'So we can now go round officially and pay our respects.'

'I'll get shaved,' Clegg said. 'Will you mash that when it's boiled?'

Clegg, on his way to offer condolences, carried his buckled front wheel.

'It knocks hell,' Foggy said, 'out of the dignity of the whole proceedings. You carting that damn thing. There is no place for a rusty bicycle wheel in the entire protocol of bereavement.'

'I'm not hiking back up this hill again.'

Foggy sniffed.

'When I can drop it off at Eichmann's place after we've been to Sybil's.'

'Call on him first then.'

'No. You know what Eichmann's like. It could take forever to negotiate terms. I want a replacement wheel. Nothing else. So I need me mind on what I'm doing when I start haggling with him. Else I'm liable to finish up with anything from a bag of shit to a reconditioned jock-strap.'

There was a wedding in progess as they passed the church.

Women with groceries clung to the railings, waiting for a glimpse of the bride.

West Riding Studio's Mr Crabtree sat on a gravestone scraping a stain from his suede shoe and eyeing the women's legs through the railings.

Last week's confetti was fading in the cracks of the pavement.

'Are we going to call for HIM?' Foggy enquired.

'Certainly,' Clegg said. 'Can't have him nipping round on his own. Demanding his suit. Being sympathetic but incautious. Dropping something other than one of his farts for which he's justly famous.'

'I'm going to have to speak to him about that,' Foggy promised. 'I deplore his tendency to crack open loudly at the rear end. He thinks it's humorous. Insanitary creature.'

Foggy raised his hat to an elderly female acquaintance.

'Typical Simmonite sense of proportion,' he continued. 'Makes a balls of his life but achieves almost complete mastery over his sphincter.'

They walked in silence for a moment.

'What time is it?' Foggy looked at his watch. 'Let's guess where he'll be.'

They went straight to the betting shop.

'Haven't you got a tie?' Foggy regarded Compo critically as they eased him out of the crowd of similarly Austin Reed proof men in the bare smoky room.

They hustled him into the alley.

Compo raised his old khaki pullover with great dignity to reveal what might once have been a tie now securing the waistband of his trousers.

Despite his protests they began to undo it.

Foggy dangled it tentatively from his finger and thumb.

Inside the creases, parts of it were almost clean.

They began to wind it round his neck.

He stopped struggling and allowed his trousers to fall down in a silent commentary upon the imperfections of all human endeavours.

'Cover yourself up!' Foggy snapped, watching the street in embarrassment.

They marched him towards Sybil's with his hands in his pockets. He complained steadily.

Sybil was all in black. Immaculate in a neat dress. Her hair freshly set. Smarter than they'd ever seen her.

They gaped for a second when she opened the back door.

'Everybody else brings flowers,' she said, looking at the wheel in Clegg's hand.

He propped it against the wall.

Foggy tried to look wheel-free and blameless. He raised his hat. 'We read it in the paper,' he said.

Clegg removed his cap.

Foggy nudged Compo who nudged him back before getting the message and lifting off his own shapeless woollen cap. A movement which brought a dangerous droop to the angle of his trousers.

'We called to offer our condolences,' Foggy smiled funereally at Sybil.

'And mebbe pick up me suit,' Compo added.

They elbowed him into silence.

'You'll have to wait for that,' Sybil said. 'I haven't been through all his pockets yet.'

'We could give thee an 'and,' Compo volunteered. He grunted as the elbows found him again. He reached out to retaliate but had to change his mind quickly to recover his plunging trousers.

'If there's anything we can do,' Foggy proffered, 'please ask.'

She eyed them steadily for a moment.

'Mebbe you can tell me,' she said, 'how he died in bed

yet managed to get his slippers wet through – lipstick on his chops – and fluff all over his second best trousers.'

'It can't a bin easy,' Compo grinned.

Foggy was looking for a hole to crawl into.

'Poor old Sam,' Clegg sighed. 'I hope he wasn't wandering about or something – half delirious.'

He shook his head gravely, thinking, Sybil, you hawk-eyed, dark creature. I leave a smudge of Lily, Bless Her, on him and you're on to it. What could I do with your forty watt bulb? You should have seen him when I started.

'People's lips,' Compo explained, 'can go a funny colour when they're dead. Me grandad's went purple.'

'This looked like Passion Pink,' Sybil said.

'O me grandad's din't,' Compo continued. 'His looked like he'd bin eatin' blackberries.'

'Well it's all very queer,' Sybil glared. 'Makes me wonder if he didn't go out that night. Sneaked out. Behind me back.'

'How could he?' Clegg enquired innocently.

'That's right, he couldn't, could he?' She stared at him intently. 'Without some help.'

Under her probing eyes, he could sense Foggy shuffling guiltily. Feel his own colour rising. He hurriedly offered Compo a cigarette. Pretended to drop the pack. Compo shot his hands out to catch it and Sybil shrieked and turned away as his pants fell down.

'If you've got such a thing as a bit of string, Sybil,' Clegg said angelically.

They reassembled Compo's propriety.

'Get him covered up,' she snapped. 'I won't have him stood in my doorway showing his manners. Good God,' she said, 'who does your laundry?'

'Me,' Compo said, 'but I must admit I an't got the touch.'

'Touch?' she spluttered. 'You look as if you've missed 'em altogether.' She began closing the door. 'You might find some string in the shed.'

'And we'd appreciate it,' Clegg said, 'if we could just pay our respects to Sam as well.'

'Aye, well you can do that as well,' she said. 'Because that's where he is.'

'In the shed?'

'Why not?' She dared them to question it. 'In't that where he always damn well was? And I'm not having all his cronies tramping over my fitted carpets.' She slammed the door.

Sam on trestles in his shed. Unfussy cremation coffin. White lining. His head near his beloved lathe looking mysteriously smaller but still wearing the grin.

'No wonder she's suspicious,' Clegg said. 'She knows the poor bugger never had owt to laugh about here.'

They advanced cautiously into the small remaining spaces, into the cool, near dusk of light through the small, dirty window; into the smell of oil, wood shavings, varnish, fearful of knocking tools and shed paraphernalia into the coffin.

'Where's his lid? He'd be safer wearing his lid,' said Compo.

It was on the floor. Along with lengths of Sam selected timber.

'He din't ought to be in here,' Compo said. 'He ought to be int best room.' He took his tie from round his neck and wound it back round his trousers. 'Tha dun't need a tie in here. I'm sure. I thought tha said this were going to be formal.'

'Naturally, we assumed it would be.'

'Typically Sybil,' Clegg said with a note of begrudging admiration. 'Unorthodox but practical.'

'He din't ought to be left out here.'

'Let's face it,' Clegg said, 'he's not going to be bothered by draughts. And if it's security you're worried about – who's going to pinch him?'

But they were all offended on behalf of Sam.

'She's wearing black for him. Mebbe she thinks that's enough.'

'I must say she looks quite smart.'

'Mebbe Sam would have stayed home a bit more if she'd worn them sort a stockings more often.'

They stared at the candlefat features of the corpse.

'Does tha suppose he knows what's going on?'

'It looks bloody boring being dead,' said Clegg.

They heard Sybil talking outside. They pushed open the door a fraction. Saw her in conversation with two men in overalls.

'It's their kid,' Compo said. 'Sam's brother Colin and a mate.'

Sybil pointed to the shed. The men started to walk towards it.

'Come to raise stink I'll bet,' Compo grinned, 'about their Sam being dumped in here.'

'I'm glad you lot are here,' Colin said. 'You can give us a hand out wi' Our Kid.'

'I should think so,' Compo said.

He was a much younger, slimmer version of Sam, with a face like a mournful horse.

'An' if you wun't mind holdin' him out there a tick,

while me an' my mate here get that lathe out.'

My Mate was younger still. He had a beer belly and a podgy unshaven face. He lit a Park Drive.

'He left thee them tools an' all, din't he,' he reminded Colin. 'I should have them while you're at it.'

'He left me the lot,' Colin said with the air of a man of substance.

My Mate ran his piggy eyes rapidly over Sam's gleaming tools. Flakes of his ash fell into the coffin.

They took Sam out into the garden. Set him up on his trestles again, behind the shed, away from the road.

'I'll blow the ash off him,' Clegg gasped, 'when I get me breath back.

'Yes,' panted Foggy. 'Did you notice? There was one tricky moment there when I thought they were going to help us.'

They heard the sounds of inheritance ripping the shed.

'He'll have an oil stone somewhere,' Beer Belly said. 'Have you looked in that drawer?'

'It's stuck.'

'Here, let me have a go,' volunteered Beer Belly.

There was a noise of brute force and they braced themselves against the outside walls as the shed trembled.

An aphid settled on Sam's nose. Folded its wings clumsily and began to walk downhill.

'Get it off,' Foggy said.

'Thee get it off,' Compo said. 'I don't like touching him.' He waved his hands in explanation or perhaps sheer exuberance at his freedom from falling trousers. 'Not now he's cold,' he said.

Foggy tutted his disapproval, pointed his lips and bent down to blow across Sam's face.

Unnoticed, Compo lowered his own head stealthily

and shouted in Foggy's ear. 'BOO!'

Foggy leaped a foot into the air, his hand clutching his palpitating heart.

Compo cackled delightedly.

'You bloody moron,' Foggy accused.

'Did tha see him?' Compo asked Clegg. 'He thought for a minute Owd Sam had reared up and nipped his bloody ear.'

'I thought no such thing,' Foggy protested sheepishly. 'It's purely a reflex action. All you succeeded in doing was demonstrating the fine tuning of a lightning reaction pattern that kept me alive in Burma.' He straightened his tie and brushed his lapels fussily.

'I should think so,' Compo hooted. 'One bang an' I bet tha were acrosst nearest border into . . .' He paused uncertainly. Drifted into one of his foggy expressions. He looked at Clegg for help.

'China,' Clegg said.

'China,' Compo repeated.

The aphid, phlegmatic creature, was strolling unperturbed towards Sam's eye.

'Dozy little pillock,' Compo said. 'Must think Sam's a plant.'

'They secrete honey,' Clegg announced. He looked at Compo. 'From a gland at the rear end. Which is more, by God, than can be said for you.'

Compo eyed the moving particle with new respect.

'And what's more,' Foggy said, 'they do it quietly.'

'It's not all that clever,' Compo pronounced, 'when tha thinks what a mess it must mek of their underpants.'

Perhaps offended by this last remark, the creature opened its wings with the same general air of incompetence and as they watched, launched itself giddily into the vast, unfriendly air.

The shed door opened with a smack as Beer Belly backed out grunting under the weight of his end of Sam's small lathe.

They watched the pair manhandle it into the back of a van.

'He's all sentiment is their Colin,' Clegg said, 'and that bugger with him.'

But at least there was more room for Sam.

Practically all they'd left was the coffin lid.

'What's she going to do wi' this shed?' Beer Belly asked, poking the wood as his made his last, thorough inspection. 'She'll not be needing it now all this stuff's gone.'

'I never thought to ask,' Colin said.

'Never mind,' Clegg said, 'you'll soon pick these things up.' He smiled at Beer Belly. 'You're in good hands.'

'This lot'll tek down tha knows,' Beer Belly pushed in demonstration at the walls. 'I could borrow a roof rack.'

'Hey up!' Compo pointed at the coffin. 'Tha's not plannin' on leavin' him in the bleedin' garden.'

'Not now, you stupid get,' Beer Belly said. He turned to Colin. 'I could have it away while you're all at the funeral. So's not to distress anybody like.'

Foggy sniffed incredulously.

'It'll be Monday,' Colin said. 'You'll be at work.'

'If I can't have an hour off,' Beer Belly said, walking Colin to the van with an arm round his shoulder, 'to do a mate a favour during a bereavement, it's a poor bastard lookout.'

'Check your pockets,' Foggy suggested.

107

They watched them drive off. The old van squatting down on her wheels at the back like a cat over its toilet.

They carried Sam back inside.

They looked at the effect and carried him out again and borrowed a sweeping brush from Sybil.

As they swept the place out she watched them from a window, fiddling with the single string of imitation pearls she was wearing on her black dress.

He looked better when they left him.

Even if he was lying there unSamlike, quietly gathering a layer of fine dust.

They forgathered early that evening at the Three Legs. Unofficial mourners at an unofficial wake.

Compo, Foggy, Clegg and Lily, Bless Her in a smart two-piece and Sid who could only stay for an hour before departing on his rounds for the chipless deserts of the outlying villages.

In honour of the occasion, they started on shorts.

'Well I think it's awful,' Lily, Bless Her said, 'a shame him lying there.' She wiped the gin daintily from her lips with a corner of a lace handkerchief about the size of a matchbox label. 'Shed – the bitch. Does she think the earth would tremble if she opened up that front room? It's psychological somewhere. Keeps it as tight shut as her legs.'

Foggy choked a bit hereabouts on his vodka.

'And if you'll listen to a professional opinion,' she continued, 'that's about as shut as you can get. Oh she kept him clean. I'm not disputing that. But she kept him at a distance. It's funny in't it. She couldn't abide his underpants but yet she could poke cheerfully into drains in the name of housework. You can't understand 'em.'

'The unclad male's not all that irresistible,' Clegg suggested, 'to somebody raised on Ovaltine adverts and the *Christian Home Journal*. Especially round here where he's liable to be half clad anyway.'

He went away and came back with another round.

'You know what local male bedroom regimentals are round here. The nervous bride gets second best of both worlds. Not just baggy wollies but bits of skin poking out. And hair.'

'I see Yorkshire's not doing too well again in the County Championship,' Foggy said.

Clegg ploughed on undeterred. 'It must be a hell of an awakening – or at least it must have been in Sybil's day – that first magical flannelette night; even to regular readers of *Picturegoer*.'

'True.' admitted Lily, Bless Her, 'but when you've seen one unstreamlined bedroom dangling male, you've seen 'em all. You're entitled to a good laugh first time and get it over with. Damn it, you can't go through life laughing at the same old joke. They don't try, some women,' she accused. 'If they'd persevere they'd get so's they hardly noticed.'

'Is that it then?' Sid asked in protest as he brought in another round. 'Is that the highwatermark of marital relations then? Is that the paradise that's promised? Just keep at it and you'll get so's you'll hardly notice.'

'It's not for me,' winked Lily, Bless Her, 'to be advocating widespread marital harmony. I've got a trade to keep.'

'My missis din't last long,' Compo sighed. 'She ran off wi' this chuffin' Pole. He used to kiss her hand, silly bugger. And he only worked for Huddersfield Corporation.'

109

'I once achieved,' confessed Foggy, 'a predominantly spiritual affinity with this lady, relief manageress of the NCO's NAAFI at Oswestry during the war.'

He raised his glass and drank a silent toast. 'The one with the glasses.'

'Tha'd be all right for thee Eccles cakes there then,' Compo cackled wickedly.

'Bog off,' Foggy told him. 'It was a relationship without sordid blemish.'

'I've never had anybody but my Old Lass,' Sid confessed with what started out to be a tone of pride but ended tinged with regret as he studied Lily. 'An' I have to put so much spade work into getting her it's sometimes an anticlimax when it happens.' He sipped his whisky reflectively. 'And once,' he continued, 'when it was all over I found I'd missed Match of the Day.'

'You can't be too careful,' Clegg agreed.

'I sometimes wonder if it's worth it,' Sid went on. 'Present company excepted of course,' he said, smiling at Lily, Bless Her, gallantly.

'You're welcome,' she said, giving him the full smile.

'Gawd,' he said, and 'No,' to Clegg who was passing round the drinks which Foggy had just bought in. 'I'll have to be on me way. I'm chippin' tonight.'

'Get it down you,' Clegg said. 'It'll keep the draughts out up them hills.'

Subconsciously Lily, Bless Her, adjusted the frills of her blouse more decorously about her breasts.

They all drank deeply.

Later, when the singer was belting out a Shirley Bassey number with not quite enough drama to disarrange her aluminium hair;

when Foggy was swaying slightly through a personal thought-train which was taking him back along a road to Mandalay and the taste of rice wine;

when Compo was using two glasses for binoculars and thinking – Mew could sing like that – ret loud;

when Sid's professional conscience was speaking to him moodily of anxious, hungry souls awaiting the sounds of his motor among the chipless hills;

when Clegg was counting the empties on the table with an air of quiet seriousness and mild surprise;

then Lily, Bless Her, began to weep softly at the thought of Sam neglected.

Four pairs of hands reached out immediately to offer comfort.

'At least if I had him,' she said, 'poor bugger, he could have me best room.'

And looking back afterwards they saw that it all began when Compo said to Lily, Bless Her, 'Don't fret theesen, lass. It's our fault. We took him back to her. Bloody Sybil. Well don't thee fret theesen. If we took him to her, then we can fetch him back again.'

And they were just far gone enough for it to sound almost reasonable.

'I'd have him,' she said, 'and welcome.'

She dried her tears and gave Compo a grateful hug so naturally they were all keen to get in on the act.

'I'll keep him decent till they come for him on Monday. Candles and things.'

She began to cheer up rapidly as she developed her plans for decorating Sam.

'Flowers. He ought to have flowers. And a low, artificial light. You could make him really attractive.'

'I doubt if Sybil would miss him,' Clegg pointed out.

'She's all dressed up too smart for visiting sheds. So as long as he was back in time for his funeral . . .'

'As a tactical exercise I'd say it could be done.' Foggy began to move glasses to demonstrate the plan. 'Of course the key factor – is transport.'

They all looked at Sid.

Bass notes of foreboding rumbled in his belly. A figure of retribution hovered through the fumes in his head both menacing and Ivylike, but vanished and gave way before Lily, Bless Her's tear-bright, appealing eyes which were fixed on his face and waiting for his answer. Her hand played nervously with the frills across her chest.

He swallowed.

'All right,' he said. 'But you'll have to wait til I've been round chippin'.'

'Fine,' Foggy said. 'It'll be dark then.' He raised his glass. 'You're a gentleman, Sidney.'

'Aye he's a good lad,' Compo said.

He's a twat thought Sid, but found himself embraced by Lily, Bless Her, being clutched fiercely to the soft scented and entrancingly springy matrix of her ample charms.

Her lips tasted deliciously of gin.

'Hey up a minute,' Compo protested, 'it were my idea.'

Lily had work to do so they went back to Clegg's and watched Match of the Day while waiting for Sid.

This had a particular fascination for them on Clegg's old set which distorted everything in the lower half of the screen.

Fractured legs at incredible angles.

Made knees appear to have been assembled backwards.

It lent a new dimension to the game.

They dipped into a crate of ale steadily in an attempt to keep sobriety at bay, afraid of what it might make of the night's work they had to do.

'We shall know when we're pissed,' Compo said, 'when this bastard picture starts looking straight.'

He rubbed his eyes and shook his head. 'I don't know how tha stands it.'

'I find Come Dancing best,' Clegg said. 'Whenever I'm depressed I have a look at that and within minutes I'm nearly suicidal.'

The time dragged slowly but with the combination of ale and nervousness they were able to keep themselves occupied going for a pee.

'He's had second thoughts,' Foggy said. 'He's sloped off home, the sod, and I don't really blame him.'

But he hadn't and they could have killed him.

He came in large as life and reeking of chips and mental confusion and fell on the rest of the ale eagerly.

They drove the van slowly along Hillcrest View. They parked outside the bungalow next to Sybil's.

Sid switched off the engine and the lights.

They sat there, nervously, listening.

There was a noise like feet on gravel.

It was Compo crunching through a piece of fish.

'For Christ's sake,' Sid said, 'are you still stuffing your face?'

'They're only scraps,' Compo protested indignantly. 'Send us a bill. I'll pay for the bastards.'

There were still several living room lights on in the street, but Sybil's was in darkness.

A dog was barking nearer town.

Foggy warmed his shivering buttocks against the pans.

They stayed there, delaying the inevitable, breathing beer fumes till the windows steamed up.

The street remained quiet.

No psychic tremors of their purpose appeared to have disturbed the urban calm.

They wiped the windows.

Clegg finally opened his door and broke the spell.

They disembarked quietly into the cool evening air.

'Do you all have to get out just 'cos I got out?' Clegg complained. 'I was only going for a pee. I'm busting.'

They discovered that they all were.

They looked around for promise of relief.

There was nothing but knee-high walls and miniature shrubbery.

A pox on your new estates, thought Clegg, his spirit yearning for something vernal, lush, Victorian.

They climbed back in the van and drove with vigour to the Council facilities in Finkle Street.

They went down the steps at speed.

Frightening the life out of two drunks who were trying to weigh each other on a broken machine.

'It wasn't us,' whimpered one of the drunks as they clattered past. 'It were broke when we came. Ask my mate here.'

He turned seeking confirmation only to find that his mate was nowhere to be seen.

He began to call plaintively.

'Ronnie! Ronnie, are you there? O God, you've knocked him down.'

He examined the tiled floor which was Ronnie-free.

'What have you done to him?'

He brightened. His face spread into a slack-mouthed grin.

'Is it a trick? Go on then, I give in. Show me, tell me how you do it. Come on. Don't be miserable. Tell us how you do it.'

They heard the sound of Ronnie being sick in a cubicle.

'That's bloody marvellous,' the drunk said, slapping Foggy on the back and causing some nasty steering problems.

He lurched towards Ronnie's cubicle and leaned against the door.

'Oh Ronnie,' he said, 'your mam will be disappointed.'

They parked the van in the same place, and this time disembarked immediately.

Among the lights of the town below them, Clegg could just make out the shape of the church tower near his home. He felt a pang of tenderness for his little house.

The lights in Hillcrest View appeared unchanged.

There were a few cars parked.

'Remember the gate squeaks,' Foggy warned. Thinking – why didn't I go to Australia after the war? I had every opportunity. I could have transferred to the Aussie army. Been retired now with me feet up in some sub-tropical outpost with a few select friends. Instead of shivering out here with these potty bastards, bent on dubious schemes.

He elbowed Compo.

'You and your big mouth.'

'Don't you start,' Compo said. 'They were only bloody scraps.'

'Keep 'em quiet,' Sid pleaded. 'Else keep 'em apart.'

He opened Sybil's gate. Concentrating ferociously on willing it not to squeak.

They vanished inside.

Four pairs of ears intent on Sybil-detecting could hear no sound.

The shed was unlocked.

They slipped inside, closing the door after them.

They shook Compo out of his jacket and stretched it across the small window.

Sid switched on his torch.

He gave a little yelp of fright.

Three different hands went flying to his mouth.

'O God,' he said, 'he's laughing at us. Look at him. He knows.' He pointed weakly towards Sam's grinning face.

'You silly bugger,' Compo said. 'He's allus like that.'

'He was never like that when I knew him,' Sid protested, playing the light gingerly across Sam's face.

'I don't know what the hell he's got to laugh about – he's dead, in't he.'

'It's improved his disposition,' Clegg said.

Compo was shivering. 'Hey up. Why has it got to be my jacket that goes on the window?'

'Because it was all your brilliant idea,' Foggy told him. 'Big mouth.' He imitated Compo's soothing Lily-tones. 'Don't thee fret theesen, love.' He elbowed Compo and grunted as he got one back. 'We'll fetch him back.'

'Well it's not right, ' Compo pointed to the coffin. 'Sam lying here in a shed. Saturday night. What a way to spend your last bloody weekend.'

Clegg took his end of the coffin. 'Let's get going.' He nodded to Foggy. 'Catch hold.'

'Catch hold of what?' Sid enquired. 'Where do you think you're going wi' that thing?'

Clegg looked uncertainly down at his hands on the coffin handle. 'What's wrong?'

'What's wrong? I can't get all that in the van. It's not a bloody artic. We can't tek the coffin.'

They stared at Sid.

'Well think about it,' Sid said impatiently. 'What's to stop Sybil having a look through the window tomorrow? It's asking for trouble if she can't see a coffin.'

'It's true,' Clegg admitted mournfully. 'She might just peer in to have a laugh at him.'

'Course it's true,' Sid went on. 'We can't just swan off with the bloody lot.'

'Are you suggesting,' Foggy enquired, 'that this expedition hasn't been properly planned?'

'It's a shambles,' Sid said.

'I was just about to mention,' Foggy said huffily, 'the desirability of not taking the coffin.'

'You want locking up, you lot.' Sid had an awful premonition. 'And I'm sure it'll happen.'

'All right,' Clegg said. 'If we've got to get devious about it then devious we'll get. But it's a bugger,' he added, 'if you can't do a favour for a mate,' he looked at Sam, 'without having to leave a trail of deception.'

Something about Foggy's actions drew their attention. They watched as he cocked his head and frowned suspiciously.

For a second he had the profile of a questing gun dog then his backbone seemed to crumble.

He slumped into a posture of complete dejection and covered his face.

'It's happened,' he croaked in a voice of despair. 'The one thing I've been dreading all evening.'

He reached out and thumped Compo accusingly. 'He's farted again.'

'It's the beer,' Compo explained.

They scattered for the door, and silken lungfuls of the cool night air.

Clegg pushed them round the corner of the shed.

'Don't stand in that doorhole,' he whispered, ''Cos any minute now that coffin's going to empty and Sam's liable to trample us to bloody death.'

'It in't that bad,' Compo said encouragingly.

'Go and stand over there,' they told him.

A tanker went through the High Street below them, its air brakes spitting angrily at the traffic lights.

They waited as long as they dared.

'We'll have to go back in,' Sid whispered.

'After you.' Foggy said.

'You're supposed to send in a canary,' Clegg said. 'And if the poor little sod turns green you back out again, promptly.'

They crept back in, breathing on tiptoe; surprised to find Sam still smiling.

'It's all this keg beer,' Compo explained.

'Shut up.' Foggy told him. 'If it happens again, we'll put a sodding match to it.'

Clegg appointed Compo to his station. 'You get his feet,' he ordered.

Sid took the middle.

The others gathered at the shoulders.

They remained poised uncertainly for a moment before reaching into the coffin.

Sid switched off his torch.

They took hold of their respective portions of Sam, flinched and let go again.

'Urgh.' Compo said. 'His feet are cold.'

'Get on with it,' Sid ordered, thankful for the darkness which concealed his own timidity.

They clenched their teeth and lifted Sam out of his box.

He came like a treat.

'It's easier,' Compo announced, 'now he dun't bend so much. Hey up,' he added, feeling a piece of material, 'what's he wearing? I hope it in't my suit.'

They sent Foggy ahead to act as scout.

He immediately revealed the depth and thoroughness of his military training by reverting instinctively to a manner of great officiousness.

He confused them completely with a variety of dramatic signals, then disappeared into the night.

Extremely conscious of the elementary error of showing his silhouette against a light skyline he dropped to the ground in the classic posture as recommended in the infantry manual.

Which was unfortunate, because, assuming he'd gone ahead, they fell over him on the lawn.

He was displeased to find himself lying under Sam and managed to indicate this by a series of further signals.

They had all managed to suppress their voices but many a grunt had occurred and they stayed down until they were sure that Sybil wasn't stirring.

Then a further danger loomed in the approach of the inevitable, nocturnal pet walker. He came on crooning to his beast imbecilically.

They pressed their faces and Foggy's into the damp and acrid grass.

'Never mind the lamp,' Pet Walker said. 'Just do your bizzy – there's a lamb. Do you best now pet, come on. Then we'll go back and see if Mamsy's done your boiled egg'.

Dadsy walked on.

They picked up Sam and scuttled to the hedge.

They peered after Dadsy.

They saw his shape fading as he walked out of a cone of lamplight. The pet was nowhere in sight.

'What's he walking then?' Compo enquired.

'Figure it out,' Clegg suggested. 'Whatever it is that craps on pavements and lives on boiled egg.'

'Go.' Foggy signalled, reasserting his authority again.

They scurried over the few, dangerous yards of pavement. Foggy had the van doors open. They whipped Sam inside and pulled the doors to again.

Sam refused to go in the cupboard this time.

They laid him gently on the serving counter.

'You'll have to hold him, that's all,' Sid said. 'Mek sure he dun't roll off.'

'I've left me jacket,' Compo said. 'I'm supposed to gain a suit an' all I've done is lose me jacket.'

'Keep calm,' Sid told him. 'Don't split your knickers. We've got to go back to the shed.'

They looked at him.

'As soon as that dog walker's come back.'

'What for?'

'To make things look right if anybody peeks in.'

'Who's going to be creeping round there at this time a night?'

'Well there's us silly buggers for a start.'

'Listen,' Sid declared firmly. 'I'm in enough lumber at home already wi'out getting caught for this one. I am not repeat not leaving an empty coffin lying about for somebody to find and start screaming. I promised Lily I'd transport Sam for her and so I will. But while he's away, mate, I want a substitute in that coffin.'

They shied away like startled horses.

'Who's going to lay in there, do you think?'

'I don't care. Long as he lays still and dun't get caught bloody smoking. That's up to you lot.'

Their thoughts turned instinctively to Compo.

'Piss off,' he said. 'I lent me jacket. Na somebody else can do a bit.'

'It's the kind of job you've been looking for all your life,' Foggy said. 'All you've got to do is lie on your back.'

'What about thee on the lawn? Tha's the expert?'

'It won't be for long,' Clegg pointed out persuasively. 'We'll call and see old Fairburn at the Co-op Tailoring. He'll lend us a dummy and we'll bring it straight back here.'

'Don't let's be here all night,' Sid said. 'You'd better draw for it.'

He took a pack of drinking straws from the pop cupboard.

They kept very quiet as Dadsy walked Mamsy's poodle past.

'Boiled eggs!' Compo snorted.

They locked the van and tiptoed back to the shed.

Compo put his jacket on. Sid broke a piece from one of the three straws and held them out for selection.

'It's either this else I'm bringing Sam back in.'

They were very tempted to settle for that.

'Nay come on,' Clegg said. 'It's for Sam.'

Like hell, thought Sid, having visions of Lily, Bless

Her. We all know who it's for.

Foggy drew the short straw.

He elbowed Compo for giggling.

'It's not funny,' he said, staring at the coffin.

'Tha's well out of it,' Compo said. 'Cushiest job a the lot. It's us has to be risking life an' limb cartin' bodies about. Besides tha's not lookin' well. It'll suit thee.'

They could feel him trembling as they lowered him in.

'It's cold,' he complained.

They heard his voice plaintively as they crept from the shed. 'Don't be long.'

They closed the door.

He shivered, as he was left with the night sounds and a deathly chill.

O God, he prayed, don't let me catch anything on these sheets. I bet they're not even aired.

He heard the van start up and drive away.

'Don't go past the police station,' Clegg shouted in Sid's ear. 'Take her round Belmont way. That's quiet.'

'It ought to be,' Sid yelled back. 'It's half way to the Outer bloody Hebrides.'

But he turned in that direction.

They left the street lights behind and began to climb.

Half a moon showed her severed self intermittently between clouds. Sid's lights brought moths into their path, their eyes glittering.

Sam rolled about a bit with their motion but kept patiently quiet.

They were on level going again, a B road between fields, when the engine began to cough.

'It's nowt,' Sid reassured them. 'Bloody petrol feed. She's temperamental about grit in her fuel. If she dun't clear herself I'll fix it in a jiffy.'

He dabbed the pedal a few times ineffectually.

She spluttered a few more times, then died.

They rolled quietly into a lay-by.

It was very quiet except for the wind.

A car picked them out with its lights, grew larger and passed.

'Best get him out of sight a minute,' Sid nodded at Sam.

He climbed out and came round the back.

They put Sam on the shelf above the serving hatch. It was scarely wide enough but he would wedge in at least while they were stood.

'I used to come here wi' me ferrets,' Compo said. 'On the owd bike.'

'What were your ferrets doing on the owd bike?' Clegg enquired.

They listened to the rise and fall of Sid's obscenities as he fiddled with the engine.

'I could do with a widdle,' Compo confessed.

'Let's mek it a twosome,' Clegg suggested.

They went behind the hedge. Sid followed.

'She should be all right now,' he said, wiping his hands on an oily rag. 'You should have reminded me about this before I got mesen clarted up. Hell of a place to be leaving fingerprints.'

They were illuminated clearly in a car's headlights.

The driver tooted cheerfully. His passengers waved.

'Ignore 'em,' Compo sniffed. 'Common as muck.'

The lights of the town sparkled below them.

They tried to take a bearing on Sybil's place. Compo fell about at visions of Foggy encapsulated.

They went back to the van.

Their bowels turned to water. Another vehicle had cruised into the lay-by and was parked without lights behind the van.

It was a police car.

It squatted there gleaming in the moonlight. The driver was examining Sid's van.

He turned when he heard their feet scrape. They heard his observer answering a call on the radio. The canned and neutered voices escaped through the police car window.

It's going to be a right laugh, this is, Clegg thought. Trying to explain this lot. Enter Norman Clegg – Fiend.

Pickings, thought Sid, are about to become slim in the chip trade. Not to mention marital relations.

I'll tell him we just brought Sam out for a ride, Compo decided. He used to like to come here. I know it's sentimental but what can you do? Five bloody years he decided.

The driver flashed his torch across them.

'I thought it were your wagon, Sid,' the policeman said. 'Have you started chipping up here then?'

'I thought I'd give it a try.' Sid leaped into the opportunity with both boots. 'Catch the late night car trade.'

'Money grabber.' The driver got back into his car. He started his engine and switched on his lights. 'We'll be back this way in half an hour. Save us a couple a fish.'

He rolled the car steadily into the highway. They watched weakly as it gathered speed.

'Phew,' said Compo.

'Phew bloody nothing,' pointed out Sid. 'It's not over yet. I shall have to light me pans again now. We'll have to be here when he comes back.'

'Well at least we can hide Sam somewhere safe.' Clegg

refused to be depressed again after their reprieve. 'I don't ever want another shock like that. Bugger this living for kicks larks.'

'Just pray,' Sid said, 'that he dun't radio all his mates. I don't want to be up here half the night tossing fish to the constabulary.'

They decided the time had come for Sam to have a trip behind the hedge.

But first, Sid put a light to his pans.

'They're buggers the fuzz,' said Sid, 'for finding hospitable warm spots on windy nights.' He sprinkled a pinch of salt in his pans.

'Put me a haddock in,' Compo said.

They lifted Sam down from his shelf. Got him halfway out of the van when headlights began to sweep the road.

For a moment they panicked and tried to move Sam in three directions at once. Then a simple instinctive fear took charge and moving with all the lithe grace of hysteria they shoved him back on his shelf again.

The car went past.

They breathed again until they heard the squeal of brakes.

A noisy gear change and the car reversed towards them, its engine revving erratically.

'There you are,' the driver said to somebody inside. 'I telled thee. It's a chip van.'

They covered their eyes as the car was driven badly into the lay-by and parked ahead of them. Its lights and engine were turned off and music began to issue from it.

The front passenger door opened. A tubby figure staggered out and caught its balance by clutching firmly on to the car roof.

A woman's voice snapped angrily.

'Stay where you are,' ordered Tubby, waving his hands expansively and losing his balance again. He swayed like a sailor negotiating a heaving deck. 'My round,' he said. 'I'll get 'em.' As if against a heavy wave, he clawed his way back to the car, where he hung a moment contentedly. 'When you're out with a Pendlebury,' he said, performing the tricky manoeuvre of taking his wallet from his back trouser pocket, 'the evening is a succession of little goodies.'

'Sat'day night,' Sid groaned. 'The Alcohol Express.' He showed himself and called, 'We're not open yet. Pans aren't warm.'

'Have no fear, neighbour,' Pendlebury said charitably, 'we shall wait.'

He reopened the door and slid carefully along the car until he found the hole.

He fell in.

The woman snapped angrily again. The door was closed. The music turned up and blared out into the night until it was snatched and mutilated by the wind.

The fat began to sizzle.

'I know just how it feels,' said Clegg.

They covered Sam as well as they could with newspapers.

Sid switched the interior lights on. Pulled on his apron and washed his hands at the sink.

Mamsy had given him his boiled egg.

'He's scratching to go out again,' she said. 'It's funny.'

She glared at Dadsy who was half way through the Midnight Movie.

'Are you sure he did his bizzy?'

'Yes,' he said.

He watched Rita Hayworth waiting for a kiss.

'But did you actually see him?'

'For Christ's sake,' he said, 'do you want me to start bringing it back in little bags?'

She put her coat on and got the lead. The poodle signified its pleasure and knocked over Dadsy's beer.

'Don't you dare lift a finger to that sweet, harmless thing. He can't help it. I expect he's all knotted up inside. Because you haven't the patience to walk him properly and see he does his function. There's more to it than towing him on that lead.' She put the breadknife in her pocket for protection. 'You shouldn't be dragging him. He's not a bloody trolley.'

'Put the breadknife away,' he told her wearily. 'Even if the street's full of deviants and assassins it's not going to do all that much good.'

'I'm not going out there without protection at this time of night.'

'I'll take him,' he said. 'I'll take the hairy thing.'

He walked up and down the street twice without result. He let the dog off the lead.

'All right,' he said, 'let's have some free expression.'

It ran through Sybil's gate.

He stood on the pavement trying to call it back in whispers ineffectually.

'Come here boy. Here boy. Here boy. Come here you curly French poof.'

It ignored him and began digging the grass.

He tiptoed in and clipped the lead on it.

'Constipated prat,' he said.

He saw the shed.

Street rumour had it that the Mordroyd woman was using it to house her dead.

Ridiculous.

Curiosity drew him to the small, square window.

He stood until his eyes became accustomed to the faint light. Gradually he made out the shape of the coffin.

Foggy woke up and sat up and looked at his watch.

Dadsy fainted quietly where he stood.

Foggy heard the small thump and held his breath. He heard the dog whimper. So that was it? He relaxed.

The dog went home trailing its lead.

'And one no peas,' Pendlebury said, his moon face on a level with Sid's serving hatch, his eyes sliding about disobediently despite his attempts to bring them back into focus.

He squinted up at Sid. 'And give us four fish cakes. And keep the change. And have you any prawns?'

'Listen, Fartface,' Sid leaned over the hatch. 'It's gone midnight on a lonely road. What do you want? Topless waitress and a bloody cabaret?'

'Right,' said Pendlebury. 'Four no prawns.'

He gasped as Sam's arm fell into view and swung like a pendulum across his face.

He did an about turn and leaned against the hatch. He shook his head a bit and swayed determinedly back struggling ferociously to pull a *coup d'état* and regain control of his frivolous eyeballs.

He caught them trying to shove it back.

They jumped back guiltily and the arm flopped down again.

They watched appalled as Pendlebury's face followed the rhythmic swinging of the arm.

'Hey up,' he said, 'what time is it wi' your clock?'

The swinging motion of his head slowed as he fought a rising nausea. He slid to his knees, cracking his chin on the hatch as he disappeared.

They secured Sam's wandering limb.

Gamely, Pendlebury hauled himself into view again. He rubbed his chin and glared at them in an aggrieved manner.

'All right,' he said. 'All right. No bastard prawns.'

Mamsy wept and hugged the poodle as she dialled 999.

'It's me husband,' she wailed, 'he's disappeared.'

It was half-past-one before they finally got Sam to Lily's, Bless Her.

She played hell.

Until she saw their faces.

'You look ten years older,' she said.

'Twelve,' said Sid. 'All thanks to Marco poncing Polo here,' he pointed to Clegg. 'He's got wanderlust.'

'I'm sure History will justify me decision,' Clegg smiled weakly. 'And if not I can always do it meself and write me memoirs.'

'You'll never guess.' Compo grinned at Lily, Bless Her. 'We've been serving chips to policemen.'

She had the front room ready.

Spick for Lily, Bless Her. Even span.

But she blanched a bit when they staggered in with Sam.

'Oh dear,' she said, 'I didn't think he'd be unwrapped.'

She pointed to the two inadequate stools she'd set up, waiting for the coffin.

They tried him on these but he began to give in the middle.

On three chairs he was better, but as Lily, Bless Her, pointed out, 'If anybody comes I shan't have anywhere for 'em to sit.'

They moved her hand-painted lance corporal and laid Sam on the piano.

His feet overhung a bit with the lid down over the keyboard and flowers in vases piled on top of it. The effect was not at all displeasing.

They stepped back and admired it.

Lily, Bless Her, stuck candles in the old brass holders of the instrument. Sid struck a match for her and she lit them.

It was like a bier.

The room by candlelight, dignified, chapel like.

It was a vast improvement on the shed.

The blue roof-light of the police car turned and blipped in Hillcrest View.

From the darker end of the street, Dadsy watched it parked outside his gate and feared to go home.

How can I, he thought, silly bitch, now she's hauled the fuzz in, and me with ghastly stories they'll never believe and no other excuse for being on other people's premises.

He shivered and pulled the seat of his trousers tackily away from his skin where the grass had been wet. Or where the bloody dog had been.

Sid went home to bed and interrogation, rehearsing Ivyproof stories of breakdowns and an evening's frustrating but honest labour.

Compo and Clegg went in search of small stones to throw at the window of one Fairburn well known for his skills with the Co-op Tailoring and Her From The Bacon Counter.

'I hate doing it,' Clegg shook his head sadly and tossed the first handful of pebbles. 'His missis is going to take some soothing after this.'

Compo slung a handful with better accuracy.

'It's not as if we're actually going to split on him,' Clegg reassured himself as he threw again. 'He'll just have to think up some reasonable explanation for us dragging him out of bed like this and hauling him down to the shop at this time of night without him being in a position to say to us nay or even arseholes.' He grunted a bit as he threw another handful.

The bedroom light went on.

Fairburn's bald head appeared groggily. He fumbled into his glasses and opened the window.

'You've got to help us,' Clegg said. 'It's Clegg and Compo, who have faithfully guarded your secret about the midsummer madness up the hills.'

'The wife asks,' Fairburn translated the viperish noises which came from behind him in the bedroom. 'If you've been drinking?'

'We need you.'

'I think she strongly suspects that you've been drinking.'

'If it wasn't crisis time – would we even ask?'

'I'm being ordered to close the window and return back to bed.'

'We need you to save our BACON.'

Fairburn wilted visibly. Solid particles of the intolerable weight of human guilt began to bear down on his sedentary shoulders. 'I'll be right down,' he said.

Before the window closed they caught a series of shrill, incredulous, piercing, female tones.

'He's tall,' Mamsy said weepily. 'He has delicate features. Too sensitive altogether,' she added, 'for that lot in the office where he works. Especially her with them kinky boots on.'

'Had he any distinguishing marks?' the policeman

asked. He was seated huge and uniformed in her tiny G-plan room.

'Distinguishing marks!' she wailed. 'Oh don't say that. He's dead, isn't he? You think he's dead. It's a body now you're looking for. I told him to take the breadknife.'

She collapsed on to the sofa.

He picked a dog hair from his tunic and moved the poodle firmly with his boot.

'They're very rarely dead, madam,' he said to comfort her. 'Usually they've just gone off with some other woman.'

She screamed and went into hysterics.

Foggy felt tense – cramped – angry – neglected – guilty – ridiculous – terrified – tobacco hungry and in need of a damn good pee.

He tried to read the hands of his watch in the feeble light.

They must have been gone hours.

He coughed furtively to clear his tubes of the dust from the shed.

Outside, the indecipherable, distant noises of the night throbbed menacingly.

He lay without comfort, listening for spiders.

The damn shed creaked continually.

Like new boots.

Every croak drawn mercilessly like a blade through the white meat of his quivering nerves.

Let us now toast absent friends, he thought. Bastards.

Probably wallowing through some funeral binge at Lily, Bless Her's.

Well, before first light, he promised himself, we're out of here, Cyril. Like a shade of the night and sod the lot of 'em.

His spirits sank even lower as he thought of Dragon

132

Sister being knocked up to let him in.

Some damn use he grumbled, giving me a key then slamming three ugly great bolts at half-past ten every night. Not as if she's under siege, damn it. Never actually seen entire squadrons of the shiftless urban proletariat lurking libidinously in her undergrowth.

But what she does have, the good woman, and let me be the first to honour it, is a pale, pink bathroom suite with matching toilet with a wide open, glossy, inviting, unchipped, desirable pan.

He crossed his legs in his coffin and groaned.

'I switched the alarm off, didn't I?' Fairburn paused absentmindedly.

'If tha din't,' Compo said, 'there's going to be a right kerfuffle in a minute.'

They pushed open the solid Co-operative door and stepped into the Menswear Department with its smell of new clothing, furniture polish and stale air.

There was ample light from the street. Too much for security. They kept well back from the display windows and followed Fairburn into the back of the premises.

He raised a trap door and they went down worn wooden steps into a chilly atmosphere, a smell of mouldy cardboard and rising damp.

Fairburn closed the trap and switched on a single, unclean, naked bulb.

They were in a dank Aladdin's cave of former Co-operative glories. Abandoned artefacts of the windows of previous generations.

It was a kind of tailor's graveyard.

Idiot, grinning faces of yesterday's window dummies were posturing, lying or propped among the other paraphernalia.

'Take your pick,' said Fairburn. 'I only hope it's been worth it.'

Compo and Clegg moved repelled and fascinated among the plaster inhabitants.

They were all shockingly, though at least in their Southern hemispheres, indeterminately naked.

Their heads were 1920 unisex. They had startling, highly coloured coarse hair.

'I thought this were men's wear,' Compo pointed significantly to a pair of plaster boobs.

'We used to make ladies' costumes as well,' Fairburn explained. 'In the old days. When you had some craftsmen and a Tailoring Manager got to lay his tape over a wider variety of things.'

A spark began to penetrate his air of gloom.

'Even done delicately,' he said, 'the taking of a bust measurement was a wonderful thing. It brought a touch of privilege to the job. Even poetry.'

He sat down sadly on the steps.

'Not like today's dreary succession of fellers wi' inside legs.'

He sighed.

'Every day was an adventure. You never knew when a bust might not come in. Wi' that still to go at I might have stayed on the straight and narrow.'

They began selecting a dummy.

The waxy, fruit-painted skins all seemed to wear the same expression, at least among the men. Retarded gigolo.

One thing was certain.

There wouldn't be a *Doppelgänger* here for Sam.

'But they'll have to do,' Clegg said. 'If we can find one about his size and keep it well covered up. If anybody looks, they'll think the undertaker's gone expressionist.'

'They look like fairground hosses,' Compo said.

They picked their way through to a short list, which they arranged against the salt damp bricks of the cellar.

'We'll have him,' Compo pointed. 'Flossie.'

'Why?' Clegg enquired.

'He looks slightly less of a prick.'

'That's him then.'

'Do you mind,' Fairburn enquired, 'if I piss off back now for me execution?'

'I've been thinking about that,' Clegg said. 'Why don't you tell her that I'm on heart tablets, and I dropped 'em this afternoon in your fitting room. Course I din't discover this till I went to bed. So I had to knock you up, didn't I?'

'I don't like lying to her,' Fairburn shook his head. 'But it's a lot better than telling the truth.'

He shook Clegg's hand gratefully.

'I'm sorry I can't do any better,' Clegg said, deeply touched. 'But it's been a swine of a night.'

Fairburn let them out the back way.

They set off down the alley with the surprisingly heavy and naked Flossie gleaming dangerously in the moonlight.

Dadsy was still shivering at the corner of his street, stamping his feet and peering every thirty seconds at his own front gate.

What was it doing still squatting there?

Idle metallic bastard.

And what about him from inside?

Big Boots.

What was he doing?

Swilling my coffee?

Going through me Hi-Fi?

Damn it, if I was missing he didn't ought to be sitting there.

Hibernating.

They ought to be out throwing a cordon around somewhere.

Dragging the canal.

See 'em on film they're always tear-arsing about, lights flashing, sirens blowing.

The full drama.

But catch 'em for real, it's pathetic.

I could go back in. Say I've lost me memory.

Too complicated.

Say I fell down. Lying there temporarily stunned.

Bleeding to death.

Dying of exposure while she's in there stroking the sodding poodle and chatting to him.

That's it. Rub it in. Play it charitably. Stay cool.

Christ, it is cool.

Forgive them. With a sort of rueful grin.

That should twist the knife in any remaining traces of a conscience.

No chance.

He's going to want to see a wound.

Sceptical bastard.

Could clout meself briskly maybe with a quarter brick.

But he knew he couldn't.

And he knew he wouldn't dare go back now while the police were there.

The wind was wailing softly.

He remembered against his will the Thing in the shed.

It was an hallucination he knew.

What else?

But O God he hoped it stayed in the shed.

He stamped his feet again. But his shivering was more than cold.

He heard someone coming and hid.

* * *

It was a nightmare passing street lights with the four bare quarters of Flossie scandalously gleaming. They tugged and struggled, seeking shadows like stepping stones.

What Dadsy saw next made his blood freeze.

Two evil figures, God save us, carting a poor naked corpse.

He saw them flitting between shadows and coming his way.

With a squeal of terror he dived over a low wall and went to ground in somebody's shrubbery.

O God, he thought. I'll never scoff at a breadknife again.

But what can you do against the Powers of Darkness?

Against the obscene, ghastly practices which are obviously commonplace among me own native hills?

Down me own street.

Christ, and all you hear about is wife-swapping.

He heard their feet.

Their satanic fearful breathing.

He closed his eyes and held his own breath.

He mustn't look.

In case they had no faces.

Or worse – some mouldering, revolting death mask from the grave.

'Oh shit,' said one of the fiends. 'It's the bogies.'

They took one look at the police car in the street and tossed Flossie over the wall.

Dadsy screamed an appalling, heart stopping, fluid congealing, strangled gurgle as The Thing fell upon him.

He fought it wildly.

Compo and Clegg assumed, naturally, that it must be Flossie doing the screaming and clutched each other as they heard the turmoil in the bushes.

Dadsy clawed wildly to escape the ice-cold horror round his neck.

He caught a glimpse by lamplight of its awful, grinning face and shrieked again, redoubling his efforts until he broke free.

He shot over the wall and down the street just as the policeman was leaving and being seen off by a distraught Mamsy.

As Dadsy legged it past Sybil's he saw from the corner of his goggling eyes the dead man coming out for a pee. The dead man fastened his fly rapidly and bolted back inside his shed.

Dadsy legged it even faster.

'That's him,' shrieked Mamsy. 'He's coming back to me.'

She held out her arms lovingly, but Dadsy scorched past without slackening speed.

The policeman had seen the distended nostrils, the popping eyes.

'Has your husband, madam,' he enquired, 'ever to your knowledge been in the habit of administering to himself any noxious substance?' He looked at the rapidly retreating figure. 'Because he looks stoned out of his bleeding mind to me.'

A shaken Compo and Clegg retrieved Flossie as the bedroom light went on. They scrambled over the wall in time to see the police car leaving with Mamsy in pursuit.

They broke into a shambling trot and fled through the night.

They could see Foggy at the shed window.

Sybil's light came on.

They bundled Flossie into the coffin and crept off over the back gardens and away.

Sunday.

The wind continued and it remained cool.

It was a day of speculation.

Ivy was watching Sid struggling to get interested in his paper and wondering why he was jumpy.

Dragon Sister was offering theories to explain why Foggy had suddenly begun keeping the strange hours that he did.

Fairburn's wife began a chain of enquiry designed to determine finally whether Clegg was really on heart tablets.

Compo was wondering about collecting his suit.

Practically the whole of Hillcrest View was cross-checking to see if it was true that some of the noises in the night had been a certain householder, now under sedation, being returned home unwillingly by the police and refusing to give any coherent account of his disappearance.

Foggy was wondering if it was all a bad dream.

Clegg was wondering if it was the first time that Sam had ever got up in public on the piano.

Sybil was baking for the funeral with not much aid from a just arrived sister from Chesterfield who lost people frequently and regarded herself as the resident, family funebrial expert.

'You'll want some sherry,' she said.

'No alcohol,' Sybil announced flatly. 'We had enough

drunks about last night. Him Further Down had to be brought home and then tried to strangle his poodle. Now if you're not doing anything, Our Delia, will you run that vac over them bedroom carpets?'

'Anything else?'

'Yes. Don't knock it on me skirting board.'

'I'll see to all that in just a minute,' said Delia, who had some of the same stuff as Sybil in her. 'Don't rush me. First things first. It's only proper for me to have a look at him first. Where is he?'

'Where he always damn well was. Out in the shed.'

Sybil opened her oven door and tested a bun with her finger. 'His summer residence.'

'That's very unorthodox,' pronounced Delia.

'It's very convenient. It's saved me no end a mess. You should see some of his cronies. Not just boots you know. There's one of 'em lives in his wellies.'

'And what's the nature of the disposal?' enquired Delia who had been around long enough to pick up some terminology.

'The what?'

'The disposal. What's it to be? Are you burying him or cremating?'

'Cremation,' said Sybil. 'Which reminds me. Don't let me forget to put that piece of meat on. I've got mutton again. The beef's tasteless and such a shocking price.'

'A sprig or two of laurel would be nice,' Delia announced, looking around at the spotless order but absence of funeral decorations.

'We're having mint,' said Sybil in tones which made it clear that the subject was closed for discussion.

'For your walls,' Delia said. 'For decoration. They

sort of pick up the motifs of your wreaths. Speaking personally, I always like a sprig over the mirror. It's about all you can get away with these days. There's no spirit of ornament left in funerals. You can splash a bit round the coffin, but that's basically your lot. What's your Sam got round him?'

'Well he had his lathe,' said Sybil. 'Till their Colin came grabbing.'

'I suppose the shed's all right for viewing purposes,' Delia conceded reluctantly. 'If you regard it as in the nature of a private Chapel of Rest. But mine,' she added primly, 'always went from the front room. And I wouldn't have it no other way. Well, are you going to show him to me then?'

'And leave these buns to burn? You know where he is.'

Delia wobbled in funeral best shoes towards the shed where Flossie lay in state.

She tiptoed in respectfully.

She took her glasses from her handbag and began to wipe them, savouring the forthcoming treat.

She put them on.

This was better than running a vac over Sybil's carpets.

She peered down.

His features swam mistily.

They were her reading glasses. Damn.

She took them off again.

She squinted down over the coffin.

'Aw!' she cooed, ecstatically. 'I've never seen him a better colour.'

She wobbled happily back to Sybil.

It was going to be a lovely funeral. She could feel it.

*   *   *

They called for Sid after tea.

Ivy eyed the three of them on her doorstep with rank suspicion.

'He's upstairs getting changed. Come in a minute.'

She's smelled a rat, thought Clegg. He raised his hat, smiling. 'Don't inconvenience yourself. We'll see him down at the pub.'

She grabbed the fist of the first one she could reach which was Foggy and yanked him across the threshold nearly jerking his head off.

They winced, imagining the whiplash effect on his neck.

'It's no bother,' she said. 'I've told you. Come in.'

She withdrew into the recesses of her den, dragging her prey who had chanced to look back once over his shoulder, his eyes beckoning frantically for assistance.

Compo and Clegg followed uneasily.

She sat the three of them on the sofa and stood with her arms folded, watching them.

You want a strong, bright light lass, Clegg was thinking, and you want us one at a time in a smoky, small room.

They could hear Sid moving about in the bedroom.

Has he had her checked, Clegg wondered? Does he realize he might be married to Martin Bormann?

Guilty as hell, she decided. Look at 'em. Faces just like he's had all weekend. The chip world's number one tearaway. Big Sid.

She could hear him clumping about upstairs.

Like a maladjusted pony.

That was the trouble. Whatever they've got him involved in he'll stick his damn great foot through it. He's too soft.

142

They were looking at the ceiling. Sending urgent psychic signals asking Sid to pull his finger out.

'How was it,' she enquired, 'that you lot knew about Sam Mordroyd being dead before his wife did?'

They went various shades of red.

'We were very close,' Clegg said.

Foggy smiled weakly. 'ESP?'

Compo placed a finger on his nose and crossed his eyes dizzily to look at it, and with the aid of this small device he seemed to forget about everything and went off happily in his own direction.

'ESP?' she snorted. 'Sounds more like parrot pee to me. Don't come here with a tale like that.'

She sat down looking both angry and worried.

'I don't know exactly what you're doing but you're up to summat and I don't want him dragging in. You start these daft games sometimes and they end up serious.'

'Like marriage,' Sid said, padding in on stocking feet. 'Have you seen me shoes, lass?'

'They'll be taking your shoes,' she said. 'And your tie and your belt.'

They walked to the King's Head feeling depressed.

'I wish it was over,' Sid confessed. 'On top of everything else it's poisoning me sex life.' He drank some of his beer with little pleasure. 'Which was always in a most delicate state of balance.'

'We've all got problems,' Compo said. 'Look at me suit.'

'Call that a suit?' Sid scoffed. 'You look like you're wearing offcuts from bedclothes.'

'Me new suit,' Compo corrected. 'The one Sam left me. When am I going to get that?'

'Never mind that. When are you going to get a round in?' Foggy wanted to know. 'You can't save it all for the bookies.'

With almost no effort on their part, their depression steadily increased.

The thought of moving Sam again after last night's terrors was a lump in the belly that no beer could dissolve.

It seemed things couldn't get worse.

Then an Irishman rose unsteadily and sang *Mother Machree*.

When it got dark and late enough for Sam-transporting they all went with Sid for the van.

A piece of paper blew across the cinders of the waste ground.

The moon was over the disused mill.

They could hear the river running until Sid's starter began to whine.

In the entire operation that evening only one snag developed.

The van refused to start.

And who can you knock up for their kind of work at that hour of the night?

Sid worked on the engine by torchlight until it began to break light.

His put his jacket back on and admitted defeat.

'That's it then,' Clegg said. He punched Sid lightly, affectionately. 'Get off home. Thanks anyway.'

They were all chilled to the bone.

They watched Sid walking wearily away.

For him it was over.

They had a job to do.

They had to tell Sybil that Sam was on the piano at his mistress's.

They had to stop a funeral which only had a Flossie in the coffin.

Clegg blew on his frozen fingers. Rubbed his hands.

'They're bound to have some form of heating,' he said, 'in Her Majesty's prisons.'

'There's never ever been a Foggy in the nick.'

'No comment,' Compo said.

They walked together as far as the High Street.

The sodium street lights were looking paler against the gathering colours in the East.

'Too early yet,' Clegg estimated. 'Let her sleep. I'll go round about eight. No use us all going. Cluttering up her doorstep. You know what Sybil's like. She doesn't appreciate a lot of feet.'

They watched him cross the road.

He went home and changed into his best, dark suit.

If you're going to a funeral, even to throw a spanner at it, he decided, you've got to show respect.

He shaved carefully.

Put on the black tie he'd worn when his wife died.

He mashed a pot of tea nearly as black and took his mug outside and sipped it, watching the town wake to a Monday morning.

It looked like it must be a nice day.

Not that you could ever really be sure.

Nothing was certain.

He'd seen the fresh blue of morning welsh too often on its promise of a fine day.

Especially with this bit of wind.

He put his mug down on the window sill. Picked it up

again quickly and wiped its ring from the paint with a snowy handkerchief he could change in a minute. Whereas the stain on her paint would make unquiet the spirit of his wife wherever it hovered.

Nothing was certain. If hover it did.

He put the mug down on the wall, pulled from his waistcoat his grandfather's silver watch and matched its decent, fading face to the church clock's.

Quarter-past seven.

By whose time, he wondered?

Does God need a watch?

Will he be impressed by our little measurements?

He wound the old timepiece carefully. Admired the hefty, silver chain.

How often do God's minutes tick?

In lives?

Is that what we are?

He sipped his cooling tea.

The workmen's buses were grumbling through High Street.

The second waves of the daily attack would be at their breakfasts.

Dispersed in family-pack sizes.

In all these family packs of houses.

Each sending forth its cannon fodder against the hostile forces of the day.

He cupped his hands about a match and lit his pipe.

Here I am, he thought, going reluctantly to a funeral, enjoying the sun while it lasts.

Aren't we all?

'Is there any more tea?' asked Compo 'I could just do wi' a swaller.'

He was at the gate with Foggy.

Foggy too had felt the need to show respect. He was in

his best clerical grey, wearing a black tie.

'I'll get changed when I get there,' Compo explained. 'When she giz me me suit.'

'We're all in it together,' Foggy came through the gate. 'We've had a talk about it. We're coming with you.'

Clegg nodded.

To conceal his pleasure he stared at Compo critically. 'There'll be no free beer at Sybil's. It's going to be brutal, short, unpleasant and dry.'

'All I ask,' Compo explained, 'is for nobody to open his big gob till she's parted wi' my suit. If tha blabs it all first I've no chance.'

Foggy propelled him through the gate. 'Not for anything,' he said with feeling, 'would we stand for a minute between you and Montague Burton's.'

'I can get changed int shed and we can still go tut funeral even if we have to hang back a bit like.'

'Like about Huddersfield,' Clegg said. 'She'll not want us any closer than that.'

'Pity,' Compo sighed. 'I should aliked to seen him buried.'

'Cremated,' Foggy corrected. 'As in fried.'

'That's going to be a bit warm this weather,' Compo looked up at the sun.

'Trouble is,' Clegg reminded them, 'this is going to sever relations and we promised to scatter his ashes.' He stroked his chin. 'He'll not want to spend all his death in a pot on the sideboard.'

They went inside.

He added a drop of fortifying spirit to their beakers.

'Get it down you,' he said. 'It's going to be a bugger of a morning.'

*   *   *

147

As they gathered for the funeral in Hillcrest View, Sybil was setting the dominant theme. Discipline rather than gloom.

After a good wipe of their feet at the doormat, guests were drafted to an immediate chair.

Unauthorized, free movement was rigidly suppressed.

As an alternative to the silent, hygienic tedium of the sitting room, fatigues were much sought after by the women who gravitated towards the kitchen.

At one point there were five of them buttering bread until Sybil removed the dish and replaced it with margarine.

The men got round the No Smoking rule by respectfully visiting the body in the shed, until the clublike atmosphere was engendered within its flimsy portals, and smoke began trickling out through the keyhole.

Great clouds of it enveloped the new visitor as he opened the door and pushed his way in through the crush. Eyes smarted and became red rimmed, giving rise in later years to the legend of the sentimentality of the Mordroyds.

Inside the house, Delia was leading a Mr and Mrs Knowles from Halifax through a detail-studded commentary on the interment of her most recent husband.

Colin was sporting a yellow pullover knitted by his wife under his suit, and reading *Exchange & Mart*.

God knows who had knitted the shape of his wife in the old check coat she kept wearing on account of having the Cortina to support.

Cousin Olive was causing a bit of a frost by arriving with her skirt too short and dragging with her a little feller half her size in all directions and twice her age in a shabby black Homburg whom she introduced as 'my friend Mr Zapojinsky'.

Grandad Hepworth had arrived with Paul and Nora but without his hearing aid become the focus of much polite shouting.

Sybil got the second best knives out which Sam had won in his racing pigeon days.

A Mr Humphries called from the Snap Lock Self Seal Food Refreshener Company about the complaint.

Sybil attended Uncle Jack Abdy's metal left leg with devoted care, placing him cautiously where he wouldn't be liable to chip her furniture.

They turned the corner into Hillcrest View and were stunned by the number of cars already parked near Sybil's.

'They're early.' Clegg frowned. This was going to make things all the harder.

They walked on more depressed than ever.

Passing without seeing the window where Dadsy was staring out gloomily in his dressing gown.

He looked terrible.

They stopped at Sybil's gate.

Foggy opened it slowly.

'Tha can gi' it some stick now,' Compo said.

'Force of habit,' Foggy apologized.

'We'd better check in the shed first,' Clegg suggested. 'See if Flossie's been rumbled.'

What he meant was – see if Flossie's been magically changed back to Sam. O God mend Sid his van. I know the motor's more or less past it but it shouldn't be beyond your powers to have nudged him till he fixed it, and pulled off the Flossie–Sam exchange.

They opened the door and gasped as the smoke billowed around them.

They began to cough.

A solid phalanx of funeral-suited men turned red-rimmed eyes towards them as they pushed their way in.

Immediately their own eyes began to prickle and smart.

They elbowed their way nearer the coffin.

'He looks well,' one of the men said. 'Dun't he look well?'

Well not to them he didn't.

He looked too damned much like Flossie.

They squeezed their way out again and dried their eyes.

'Where've they come from, all this lot?' Clegg demanded to know. 'It gets worse and worse. Fancy having to tell her in front of this lot. Excuse us folks, but there's going to be an unscheduled stop at Lily, Bless Her's. Just talk among yourselves while wife and sweetheart battle it out.'

'We're not saying owt,' Compo reminded him, ''til I've got me suit. I can't go to Sam's funeral in this lot.'

'Could we have a word with the undertaker?' Foggy suggested unconvincingly.

They gave him a filthy look.

'O big laugh.'

'We could throw ourselves on his mercy.'

'What the hell do undertakers know about mercy? If that got cosmically popular they'd be out of a job.'

'It's just that he's the bloke that could do it, isn't he?' Foggy's shoulders sagged. 'But he won't. Of course he won't. He daren't. O shit!' he said. 'We're on our own.'

'Ring the bell,' Compo said. 'Ask about me suit.'

Sybil answered the door.

'Oh it's you lot. I wondered if you'd hear about us

having to move the funeral forward.'

Can't keep owt quiet round here, she thought.

'They're that busy at the Crematorium you have to fit in where you can. Take what you can get.'

'Can I take me suit then?'

She glared at him as he stood there polluting her step.

'Wait here,' she said.

She closed the door except for a crack.

They could hear the subdued funeral voices inside the bungalow with occasional outbursts of Grandad Hepworth stuff.

'She was going to do it behind our backs.'

'How deceitful can you get?'

They caught a glimpse of Mr Zapojinsky through the crack, handling his Olive.

She gave him a quick hug to her adequate chest, then wagged a finger at him.

He wore an expression of great beatitude and hid it shyly behind his hat.

'Does tha suppose we'll ever get back,' Compo asked, 'to the simple things in life?'

Sybil thrust the suit at him.

'Here,' she said. 'Take it. And just think on I want that hanger back.'

The hearse and limousines arrived.

'We'd like a word with you, Sybil,' Clegg said.

'Not now,' she said. 'There isn't time.'

She went to greet the undertaker, Wolstenholme, but was overtaken by Delia.

Wolstenholme watched unhappily while Delia ran her fingers lovingly over his gleaming machine.

'Tell that freaky creature,' he whispered savagely to Little Benny Godfrey the fourth driver, 'to keep her claws off that paintwork.'

'Thee tell her,' Benny said. 'Tha's the big executive.'

'How can I tell the dozy twat? I'm supposed to be sympathetic, aren't I? With never a crack in this plummy expression.'

He turned it now on the advancing Sybil and raised his black silk hat.

'Can we stop at the dairy on the way back?' Sybil asked. 'I'm running low on milk.'

Behind the Wolstenholme façade a Wolstenholme quivered.

Sweet Jesus Christ, he decided, I'm on a right one here.

'If you can arrange to move some of these cars, madam,' he bowed, 'then I can draw up the procession.'

Delia smiled her approval.

She began fingering his chrome.

'It looks a treat,' she said. 'I wish I'd brought me proper glasses.'

'Well I tried,' Clegg said. 'You heard me.'

'So now what?'

They watched Sybil organizing the moving of the cars.

'Nothing to it,' Clegg said. 'They'll probably lynch us.'

He pointed to Wolstenholme. 'It's maybe best if we wait till he finds Flossie. Then when he calls Sybil to the shed, we can go in and confess. Then nobody else need know. They'll just have to wait a few minutes while the undertaker whips off to Sugden Street and comes back with Sam.'

'We won't have to confess,' Foggy said. 'She'll know as soon as we walk in that shed.'

'That's right. Where's Sam, she'll ask? Funny you should say that we'll tell her.'

'When they've cleared that shed, I'll change me pants,'

Compo said. 'She bin through all t' pockets. There's nowt in.'

'I am just relieved,' Foggy said, 'that their Colin cleared that shed. If there was anything sharp left in there she'd stab us.'

'That's a thought,' Clegg suggested. 'Could we blame Sam's disappearance on their Colin? Or that mate of 'is? The buggers swiped everything else.'

They watched Wolstenholme walking magnificently towards the shed.

Compo pointed to Wolstenholme's hat. 'There's allus some sod got to go one better,' he complained. 'I wait ages for me suit then up comes some turd out to steal the limelight wi' his comical hat.'

Foggy yanked Compo's pointing arm down. 'Where's your manners?' he asked. 'Just cos we're about to be done for body snatching it's no reason to be completely ape. Speaking personally,' he added primly, 'I intend to impress the jury with me quiet demeanour and military bearing.'

Wolstenholme was thinking – Shed for Christ's sake. Not content with daubing sticky fingers all over me hearse, they've actually thrown the deceased out now in the shed.

He shot his snowy starched cuffs.

Allah be praised that they didn't just have a coalhouse.

What surprises me is why they didn't just dump the poor sod out for the dustbin lorry.

He opened the shed door and staggered back coughing.

Seven men and umpteen cubic feet of stale tobacco cloud whirled past him.

He recovered his poise and went inside.

He began fanning briskly with his hat.

He wiped his eyes and when some of the smoke had

cleared he peered through his tears at the deceased.

He shuddered.

'O my God,' he said. 'Who coloured that?'

Reacting instinctively and in the best interests of his profession, he got the lid on – quick.

Tilting sharply at one corner, where it had to come down to meet Little Benny, they watched the coffin being carried to the hearse.

'Well how do you like that?' Foggy snorted. 'For professional incompetence. That's disgusting. They'll obviously bury any bloody thing.'

'Cremation,' Compo said. 'Have they finished in tha shed?'

'All right, cremate then. Either way it just makes you think. How many other coffins that you see are just full of junk? Why not? You know how slow the councils are at getting rid of stuff that's too big for your dustbin. There could be a right old racket going on here. Illegal bulky refuse disposal.'

'Typical,' Compo snorted. 'Another wangle for the rich. I'm stuck wi't council but if you've got a bob or two and know where to phone I bet tha can get thee old mangle shifted.'

They stowed Flossie gently in the hearse and arranged the wreaths about him.

'If we're going to stop it, we'll have to stop it,' Foggy said, 'before it goes any further.'

'Hold on a minute,' Clegg restrained him. 'Think about it. Don't go galloping in with your vest in a knot. This has sort of altered the whole complexion.'

He took them to one side where they formed a little conspiratorial group near the path.

'If they want to bury Flossie, let 'em bury Flossie.'

'Cremate,' Compo said.

'Shut up,' Clegg continued. 'What's it matter as long as everybody's happy? All we have to do is figure out somewhere we can pop Sam. And we're in the clear.'

'That's horrible,' Foggy protested. 'Indecent. It'd have to be up there, where we promised to scatter his ashes.'

'Right,' Clegg agreed.

'I can't dig,' Compo pointed out. 'It's me back.'

'You do as you're told,' Foggy elbowed him. 'He left you his suit, didn't he?'

'I might a known,' Compo looked disgusted. 'There's allus a bloody snag.'

Sybil was being shown into the first car, accompanied by Delia who was obscured quite happily in a full veil.

Unfortunately this further diminishing of her vision was causing her to wander.

Wolstenholme steered her back on course, and as they waited by the hearse while Sybil was settled, he took the opportunity of fingering Delia's veil and giving his chrome a bit of a rub with the trailing end of it.

'What will Lily say?' Foggy asked.

'What can she say? She can't keep him indefinitely on the blasted piano.'

Grandad Hepworth was led past.

'Who's she?' he was enquiring in a voice which could be heard in Huddersfield. 'Showing all that leg wi' yon queer little bugger?'

'Mind where you tread, Grandad,' Nora said, her face turning scarlet, 'Can't you keep his voice down?'

'Give him another biscuit,' Paul said.

'He makes crumbs. You know he makes crumbs.'

Clegg was floating visions of a simple but impressive monument. 'We can make it nice up there for him. Natural but tidy. The world would think it was just a happy accident that the grass was cut near this nameless, but tasteful stone. He'd like that. Rough but effective.'

'And I'm not cartin' any damn gret boulders about.'

'All right. All right. Awkward little pillock. Will you settle for cutting the bloody grass once a week?'

'I'm off to get changed,' he said and took his new suit into the shed.

They went with him.

They came out again when he took his wellies off and stood near the door.

'And when we're all dead, we'll leave a note,' Clegg said. 'Describing exactly where he is, and explaining everything.'

'How can we?' Compo scoffed. 'When we're all dead?'

'Last survivor does it, nig-nog. We'll make a pact.'

'Tha better write it for me then,' Compo said, struggling to get out of his pants. 'My spelling in't too good.'

'Who says you're going to be the last survivor?' Foggy enquired. 'What about that crippled back?'

They were being signalled from the gate.

There was a place for them in the cars.

They grabbed Compo.

'Come on.'

He came down the path hopping into his pants.

They were shown into the last car.

A sort of mobile doghouse, Clegg realized, looking at the ancient vehicle in relation to the glistening limousines ahead.

Wolstenholme held the door open for them.

His eyes closed under a spasm of pain as Compo entered fastening his pants.

The car already contained Cousin Olive and Mr Zapojinsky.

Compo brightened considerably at the sight of Cousin

Olive's ungainly, ageing but unquestionably prominent thighs.

'How do,' he said.

She smiled and blushed behind her rhinestone, bat-wing specs. She offered everyone a coconut mushroom.

Mr Zapojinsky raised his Homburg politely.

Clegg stared at the town passing the windows – slowly, in third gear.

Life he thought – weird.

Even the ordinary.

Perhaps especially the ordinary.

What can you make of the Hoover Repair Shop in cosmic terms?

At the consummation of the world what estimate will remain of OK Motors (Northern) Limited?

Never mind the three of us, sucking coconut mushrooms, on our way accidentally, in an old car, to the last rites for a superannuated Co-op dummy with a chip in his head from being tossed over a low wall.

He was suddenly very tired.

He caught Foggy's eye.

'It's no good, is it. We can't do it, can we?'

Foggy shook his head.

Clegg grinned ruefully. 'I thought for a minute we could wangle out of it.'

He settled back in his seat.

All right. So it was going to be painful, but proper.

And now the resolution was firm it felt already as if some of the load had been lifted.

He saw Cousin Olive and Mr Zapojinsky holding hands.

He winked broadly at Mr Zapojinsky.

Good luck to 'em.'

Mr Zapojinsky smiled shyly.

* * *

The chip van was parked near the chapel.

Sid was waiting for them, looking sheepish.

He grabbed them as they left the car.

'Hang on,' Compo protested. 'Mind me suit, and wait a minute while I help the lady out.'

They hauled him away from the view of Olive's few remaining secrets.

Sid steered them towards his van.

'Whatever it is, we haven't time,' Clegg said. 'We've got to see Sybil and stop the funeral.'

'You've time for this,' Sid said.

He opened the rear doors of the van and stepped back.

They looked inside.

Ivy stood there, arms folded, glaring down at them.

'It wasn't Sid's fault,' Clegg said. 'We got him into it. And we haven't time right now to stand here and be bollocked. I promise you, we'll come back in due time and you can have your say.'

Sid took his arm. 'Hang on a minute, blast it.'

'I reckon the blame's about equal,' Ivy said. 'You potty lot of buggers.'

She moved aside and they saw another figure in the van.

'It's another dummy,' Foggy said.

'Nay, good God,' Ivy spluttered. 'We don't want any more of 'em. I've had quite enough with this bloody thing.'

She thrust it forward almost in their faces.

They gaped at the familiar, grinning features.

Still unconvinced Clegg felt for the chip on the back of its head.

It was Flossie.

'But he's in the coffin,' Foggy said.

'No he isn't,' Sid grinned. 'Sam is.'

'But we saw him. Just now. In the shed.'

'What you saw was Sam,' Ivy yanked Flossie without ceremony back into the recesses of the van.

My God, thought Clegg. Does she handle Sid like that? He looked at her with new admiration. Powerful shoulders. A fine lass.

'Sam?' Clegg queried. 'That colour?'

'Sam.' Ivy insisted. 'With a lot of my make up on.'

Sid passed round cigarettes. They sat down weakly on the tailboard.

'When I left you,' Sid explained. 'When we couldn't start the van. I went home. She made me tell her everything.'

'I should bloody think so,' Ivy interrupted. 'Coming in half frozen at that time of a morning.'

'She got the garage out. We got the van started.' Sid went on. 'She dragged me straight round to Lily's.'

'And the less said about that one the better,' Ivy interrupted again. 'If I ever hear of you involved with her again . . .'

'I've told you,' Sid raised his hands in exasperation, 'there was nothing like that.'

'I've never seen nothing like that bloody nightie she was floppin' about in either.'

'Anyway,' Sid got back to his tale. 'We got Sam in the van. It was light but it was early. There was nobody about.'

'Piano!' Ivy sniffed.

She got out of the van and walked up and down on the pavement unable to contain her indignation.

'But when we got to Sybil's we saw that sister of her's coming out of the shed. She'd obviously seen Flossie, so we daren't leave a pale poor substitute.'

He pointed to Ivy.

'So she painted him up a bit.'

'Another fine old job for a respectable woman. If I could a got me hands on you then,' she glared at them, 'I could have killed you.'

'How did you get Sam into Sybil's in broad daylight?'

Ivy stuck her hands on her hips. 'It can be done. If you use your head a bit. Sybil was round the back. In the kitchen. The only danger was from somebody in the street. So we wrapped him in brown paper, stuck his feet in a plant pot, left some leaves showing at the top and carried him upright. Into a shed. Who's going to think twice about that?'

'Why didn't tha tell us earlier?'

'I wanted to.'

'I made him wait,' Ivy said. 'I thought it'd do you all good to sweat a bit.'

Clegg got to his feet – advanced on Ivy. He grabbed and hugged her.

'Get off,' she said. 'Silly beggar. Get away.'

He kissed her.

'I'll mek it up to you,' he said. 'In the meantime, give my love to all the other escaped Nazi leaders.'

He left her holding her cheek, blushing and flustered. She watched him walking towards the chapel.

Foggy and Compo followed.

Sid looked at her sheepishly.

'Oh get off,' she said. 'Get out of me sight.'

He ran up the steps to catch up with them.

'And mind you come straight home when it's finished,' she called.

They picked up the service at the point where the frost was thickening about Mr Zapojinsky who had been observed in the act of making the Sign of the Cross.